Chi'Raq Gangstas 3

Romell Tukes

**Lock Down Publications and Ca$h
Presents**
Chi'Raq Gangstas 3
A Novel by *Romell Tukes*

Romell Tukes

Lock Down Publications
P.O. Box 944
Stockbridge, Ga 30281
www.lockdownpublications.com

Copyright 2021 Romell Tukes
Chi'Raq Gangstas 3

First Edition March 2021
Printed in the United States of America

Lock Down Publications
Like our page on Facebook: Lock Down Publications @
www.facebook.com/lockdownpublications.ldp
Cover design and layout by: **Dynasty Cover Me**
Book interior design by: **Shawn Walker**
Edited by: **Lashonda Johnson**

Stay Connected with Us!

Text **LOCKDOWN** to 22828 to stay up-to-date with new releases, sneak peaks, contests and more...

Thank you!

Submission Guideline.

Submit the first three chapters of your completed manuscript to ldpsubmissions@gmail.com, subject line: Your book's title. The manuscript must be in a .doc file and sent as an attachment. Document should be in Times New Roman, double spaced and in size 12 font. Also, provide your synopsis and full contact information. If sending multiple submissions, they must each be in a separate email.

Have a story but no way to send it electronically? You can still submit to LDP/Ca$h Presents. Send in the first three chapters, written or typed, of your completed manuscript to:

LDP: Submissions Dept
P.O. Box 944
Stockbridge, Ga 30281

DO NOT send original manuscript. Must be a duplicate.

Provide your synopsis and a cover letter containing your full contact information.

Thanks for considering LDP and Ca$h Presents.

Acknowledgments

First and foremost, all praises are due to Allah. A big thank you to all the readers, my family, and friends. Shout to Yonkers, NY Moreno aka Smoke, love you, bro. YB, CB, Spayhoa, Smurf, Lingo, Touch, Art, Red, Baby J, and Banger. Shout out to Peeky, my guy killer. Bump, the other Barria, and TG. Shout out to my Newburg and 845 team Spice. Easy, Do-Berry, and Double-O. Much Luv to my BK guys OG Chuck, Tom Dog, K from Thompkins, Rico from Flatbush, Gonny, Tails, and my guy Skrap from Fort Green. Shout out to my BX niggas Uptown. My Harlem niggas. My Patterson, NJ niggas, Rugar, Beast, B.G., T-Burno, and all the Hats. My Chi'Raq guys Poky the Cobra, my OTF 300 niggas, and my 600 niggas. Free everybody who stood tall at hard times to only be railroaded. You will have your day. Shout out to all my D.C. niggas who was really rocking with a real New York niggas. Big shout out to Lock Down Publications the game is ours!

Romell Tukes

Prologue

The past couple of years for the notorious Chi'Raq Gangstas has been filled with a lot of ups and downs, betrayal, and expeditiously gross wealth. When the crew formed years ago as teens locked up, they had big dreams to take over the city of Chicago at any cost. After robbing, kidnapping, and murdering the city's most infamous gangstas and Kingpins Boss, Malik, and Animal took over the city.

As time went on Malik was arrested for killing two police officers but was acquitted at trial thanks to Boss and Animal kidnapping the DA's family for a ransom of Malik's freedom.

After Boss opened a car dealership to clean up all his dirty money life started to see brighter days until karma knocked at his front door.

Face and B. Stone came back in the picture trying to gain revenge to only get killed. Boss' father Ty Stone came home from prison after giving back his life sentence. Ty and his friend Smitty tried to reclaim the streets they had on lock years ago in their prime. As Ty and Smitty tried to figure out the Chi'Raq Gangstas, so was Boss' little brother Lil BD because they killed his big homie.

Boss and his crew killed Smitty's whole family and Smitty as well.

When Jenny told Lil BD that his brother was a member of the Chi'Raq Gangstas it sparked a war. Lil BD and Hitler did everything to take the crew out but they were unlucky.

Before Ty was killed, he told Boss he had a daughter, so Boss was shocked to hear he had a sister out there somewhere.

Animal was making his own plans with the help of Chole and the Colombia Cartel boss trying to take over Chicago's drug trade because she saw it as a goldmine.

When Animal tried to kill Malik, Lil BD and Hitler interfered trying to kill Boss's crew but they wasn't successful.

Boss killed King Mike his plug and his wife Rosie's brother because of a mistake he made with Animal by killing King Papi King Mike's right-hand man.

Rosie found out from her dead brother's wife that it was Boss who killed King Mike. Before Rosie could even find out the truth King Mike's wife Angela tried to kill her. Rosie fought for the gun and her life before she killed Angela. After this Rosie had to get away and leave Boss, so she left him a note and never looked back.

Lil BD found out Jenny was the one who almost killed his brother Boss. When she told him, it was Boss who killed her father Ty and that his wife was his half-brother's sister, his mind went crazy. Lil BD told Jenny the nigga she almost killed was her brother, she was shocked.

Janella the mother of Boss and Lil BD was in a car accident to only be kidnapped by unknown gunmen. Days later Lil BD was kidnapped outside of his mom's house, where he was subdued and taken away. The same night Boss was ambushed at his car dealership by a gang of masked men as he shot his way out.

Boss almost got away, but he was shot with a powerful tranquilizer that put him down. Boss was then taken away to an unknown location.

Chapter 1

Port-Au-Prince Haiti

Boss slowly woke up, he was lying face downt on the hard, cold, cemented floor. "Ahh," Boss gritted, his body was in pain as he opened his eyes trying to regain his vision to see where the fuck he was.

The last thing he remembered was getting into a massive shoot out at his car dealership before shit went black. Boss tried to recalculate what was going on as he looked around the large, high cage he was in. He could tell he was in a warehouse or some type of torture chamber somewhere.

"What the fuck?" Boss said when he saw another person moving in the far corner. It didn't take him long to figure out who the nigga was in the corner.

Boss stood up and saw Lil BD getting up looking around in a lost daze until he saw Boss on the other side of the cage.

"You bitch ass nigga you got me snatched up," Lil BD said with a malicious look on his face.

"That's the last time you call me out my name. And I don't know what the fuck's going on, nigga, I'm here with you. For all, I know you coulda set this shit up," Boss replied.

They walked toward each other in the middle of the floor. Boss saw bloodstains all over the floor and he made the quick confirmation that he was in a torture chamber, he saw chains hanging from the high ceiling and cameras in the corner of the cage so he knew someone was watching their every move.

"I wouldn't go this hard to drill your bitch ass. I woulda just killed you and finished the job, unlike somebody who didn't," BD said with a smirk.

Boss threw a right punch, hitting Lil BD in the mouth causing him to stumble backward, he caught his balance and got in a fighting stance.

"Let's get it, I have been waiting for this day," Lil BD said as he rushed Boss swinging.

Boss weaved two haymakers, but Lil BD caught him with a light jab to the chin. Boss threw a three-piece combo back and Lil BD ate the blows.

"My bitch hit harder than that," Lil BD said spitting out blood before hitting Boss with a hard, clean uppercut and left hook almost taking Boss out.

After Boss shook it off, Lil BD threw two powerful punches. Boss sidestepped to his left hitting Lil BD with two fast powerful uppercuts, knocking him on his ass. Lil BD was dizzy on the ground but he jumped back up.

"That's all you got, nigga?" Lil BD said.

Boss laughed until Lil BD hit Boss with a head blow knocking Boss to the floor. Lil BD climbed on top of Boss and started punching him in his face, like a punching bag. Boss used his strong legs to flip Lil BD over who was now on the floor trying to cover his face, as Boss pounded away at his head.

In a matter of seconds, Lil BD was able to use his feet to kick Boss off, they were going blow for blow like pro boxers.

"You done, nigga?" Boss asked, looking at Lil BD's black eye and feeling his own bruised and swollen nose on his face.

Both of them were tired as they collapsed on the ground next to each other breathing hard as if they'd just run the Boston Marathon.

"You hit harder than I thought," Boss said, making Lil BD laugh. Boss had speed knots on his face and head.

"You ain't too bad, you got that Mike Tyson punch," Lil BD returned, spitting out blood and looking around forgetting they were held captive.

"We gotta figure out what the fuck is going on. I don't even know what they drugged us with or how long we been here," Boss said as he heard a door open.

Both men stood up and walked to the gate where they saw someone coming their way clapping loud.

"That was better than Floyd's last one," a tall man said dressed in a suit now standing outside the gate smiling.

"Why are you and why are we here?" Lil BD asked.

Boss saw something familiar in the man's appearance then it came to him.

"You the Haitian nigga that had me kidnapped and let me go when I came to Haiti," Boss said.

"Yes, once again, I'm sorry about that. My men can be a little savage like at times," the tall Haitian man with long, thick, dreads stated with a handsome smile.

"Why are we here?' Boss asked

"I'll let the boss explain that but both of you are blood, we family. You're only in the cage to set your differences aside because you two need each other for what we up against," he said.

Boss and Lil BD looked at each other confused.

"Family?" Lil BD asked.

"Yes, we all we have left. We been watching you two closely. We know everything about Boss killing his father. You trying to kill his crew BD, and Boss's sister Jenny," the Haitian man said.

"Who are we?" Boss said.

"You're about to see, follow me to your private suits so you can shower and get dressed and your suits and shoes, they are all an exact fit," the Haitian man said as the cage door opened.

They stepped out more confused than when they woke up.

"How are we family?" Lil BD asked, still trying to make sense of it all.

"Your mother Janella is my sister, so I'm your uncle Luc but call me Luc, please. My father will explain everything at dinner," Luc said walking through a long narrow bright hallway full of Haitian men with guns posted up on the walls.

They got into the elevator going to the 3rd floor from the lower basement.

"The whole third floor is your place to stay. All of our maids and guards speak Creole or French a couple speaks English," Luc said as they got off on the 3rd floor entering a beautiful, private penthouse.

"Damn, this a mansion in itself," Lil BD said looking into the 40ft ceilings.

"It's three sections to this palace, we have seventy-two acres of land. I'ma be back in two hours to pick you guys up for dinner. It's nice to finally meet my nephews. Both of you are very intelligent. You will fit in with the Haitian Cartel," Luc said before getting inside the elevator were six guards awaited him.

"Haitian Cartel, mon. What the fuck is going on, Joe?" Lil Bd said.

"I don't know but we going to find out." Boss looked at the twin circular marble staircase, marble white floors, a baccarat chandelier above their head. A large antique design living room, a classy state-of-the-art kitchen, and an 18th-century French setting.

"You think we can trust or believe Luc?" Lil BD asked.

"I don't trust souls, but I do believe him. Now we just have to wait to see our purpose here," Boss said looking out the living room window to see two other stone-like buildings connected to theirs. The backyard was amazing, with manicured grass, a courtyard, a poolside cabana, a guest cottage, a Lanai overlooking pool, and acres of land stretching for miles into the mountains.

"This place is crazy, I'ma go get ready for dinner. I'ma take a show," Lil BD said.

"Do you want me to hold you down? I'll guard the bathroom for you," Boss stated.

"Nigga, this ain't prison, I'm good," Lil BD said walking upstairs as Boss stared outside deep in thought.

Chapter 2

Port-Au-Prince, Haiti

Boss and Lil BD were escorted to the courtyard behind the main mansion. Outside was tropical warm with sky blue clouds, today was a perfect day for a swim or a cookout. They were led to a tent with a long table full of food and chairs.

"Nice meeting you, my father will be out soon. I have to flyout the country," Luc said before turning to leave. "Oh, and word of advice my father is somewhat of a soul reader," Luc said laughing as he walked off with eight goons.

"What the fuck is a soul reader? He must be one of them voodoo niggas? You know this is the motherland for that shit," Lil BD said seriously loosening his tie on his Gucci suit.

Boss wore a black Armani suit. "You always overthink shit, bro," Boss said watching Haitian goons patrolling the rooftops, and outta field as if a UFO attack was to happen at any second.

"I think that's him, Boss," Lil BD said as he saw an older dark-skin man in a black tailor made suit, coming their way.

The Haitian man was medium height, with short, thick wavy hair, a gray goatee, a nice built, and hazel eyes that could pass for an orange color.

Boss and Lil BD stood up to show a sign of respect as their grandfather stepped to the table and looked at both men with his cold eyes.

"You two are my grandkids," the man said in his deep Haitian accent. "Who won the fight?" he said sitting down.

Boss and Lil BD took their seats.

"I did," Boss and Lil BD said at the same time and everybody laughed.

"Sometimes a little one on one can solve a lot of problems. Me and my brother used to do it all the time. He used to whip my ass, but I had heart just like both of you. I'm Francisque, your mother's father," he said sadly as Boss and Lil BD caught on to it.

"Why are we just now meeting you?" Boss asked.

"Because of this." Francisque pointed around the mansion. "Me and your mother made an agreement for me to keep a distance unless something was to come up."

"So, what came up?" Lil BD asked knowing something wasn't right.

"Recently your mother was captured by a cartel family for a reason I have not yet concluded but I believe she is safe," Franaisque stated in his calm voice.

"What cartel family and why would they get her? She don't know no damn cartel members, she's a school teacher," Lil BD stated upset.

"I know you're upset but there are a lot of pieces missing from this puzzle," Francisque said as he lifted his hand and moved one finger and a maid came out with a folder for him.

"This makes no type of sense at all to me," Boss said

"The Cartel family is the Colombia Cartel ran by Chole a vicious Spanish woman. Don't let her looks fool you,' Francisque said as he passed around the folder to his grandsons.

"She looks like an exotic dancer more than a Cartel boss," Boss said.

"True but you two have someone in common, keep looking through the folder," Francisque said.

Boss did as he was told and when he saw a picture of Chole with a familiar face his blood boiled like hot grease.

"He been with Chole a while before you and your crew killed her husband, Detective Rodriguez," Francisque said and Boss was hurt.

Lil BD saw the look on his brother's face and looked at the photo to see that it was a picture of Animal and Chole.

"That's crazy. So, they both had something to do with our mother vanishing?" Lil BD asked.

"I believe so, but Animal is still in Chicago building his own drug trade. He goes by the name Black now," their grandfather said.

Boss was shocked. "I shoulda known," Boss said knowing Malik was right about Animal.

"One night me and Hitler caught Animal and Malik coming out of a bar. Animal tried to kill him until we shot at both of them. I really saved your boy's life on gang," Lil BD said thinking back to the night he caught both men slipping.

"Friends always turn into enemies at some point in life. Envy is a powerful disease," their grandpa said while eating some fresh fruit.

"So, what now?" Lil BD asked.

"We get my daughter back, but we have to come as one all of us. It's the only way we will win this battle we're about to be faced with."

"We're both in," Boss said and Lil BD nodded.

"Good because we're going to Miami to kill major cartel families and frame Chole for the mayhem while we hunt our Jenelle down

"Divide and conquer type of shit. I read it in The 48 Laws Of Power," Lil BD stated.

"Yes, I have a plan. I just need both of you to be well trained and active. So, for a couple of weeks, you will both be in serious training."

"How long we been here?" Lil BD asked.

"Two days, I lost a couple of men thanks to you, Boss. But I hear you're a good shooter," his grandpa said smiling showing his white teeth"

"Sorry about that but the way they ambushed me, I thought it was an attack and they killed my assistant," Boss said thinking about how they killed Kylie.

"Now my men don't use real bullets, they're fake and they used tranquilizers for your lady friend."

"Oh," Boss said.

"Tell us about you?" Lil BD said wanting to hear about their grandfather.

Francisque spent four hours telling them about him and his life story. They were amazed at their grandfather's legacy and strength. They were proud to be affiliated with the powerful man who sat in front of them.

Romell Tukes

Chapter 3

Bogota, Colombia

Chole walked up her dirt, rocky private road on the side of her mansion leading to a barnyard and an old wooden barn shed. She was accompanied by four of her bodyguards. She was dressed in an army fatigue uniform with her long hair in a ponytail. Things for Chole were good, her drug trade was now expanding in the U.S. thanks to Animal. She was sending tons of keys to Chicago twice a month sometimes three times a month. Using the help of Victor from the Peru Cartel she was able to supply Chi-Town with the purest dope they'd ever seen. The heroin she got was causing hundreds of deaths around Chicago because the street hustlers didn't cut it the correct way.

As they walked into the empty barn full of haystacks and cattle. Chloe made her way to an area covered with old rugs and chairs. Her guards moved everything out the way to see a wood floor panel leading into the basement area which looked like a dark wide tunnel.

Once downstairs in the tunnel, they saw lights and guards posted up in the large room that was furnished with a TV, microwave, freezer, bed, toilet, chairs, and Jenelle was chained tightly to the bed.

Chloe had a tunnel built in her home a long time ago, it was her safe room that led to the highway less than a mile away.

"Nice to see you again, Janella," Chloe said, pulling up a chair next to Janella whose face showed no signs of fear or worry which made Chloe upset.

Chloe had her guards beat the shit out of Janella many times but she still remained strong.

"Let's just get this over with shit," Janella said before Chloe slapped Janella in her face.

"You don't fucking call no shots around here," Chloe spat. Janella laughed and spit in Chloe's face. "You little bitch," Chloe said, wiping the spit out her eyes. Chloe stood up and said something in Spanish.

One of her guards on the wall passed her a pocket knife as she requested. She looked back at Janella with a smile before she started to stab her multiple times in her shoulders.

"Ahhhh!" Janella cried in pain, she was unable to move because she was cuffed, so she just closed her eyes as blood leaked down her gown soaking her sheets.

"Get a nurse in here," Chloe told one of her guards who left to go get one of the maids who were all nurses as well.

"Next time when I talk, you'll shut up and listen bitch or you will starve to death."

I'm sure you have no clue why you're here and I don't plan on telling you at least not yet. You're a schoolteacher with two kids, one who recently disappeared days after you. I can't understand that but that's neither here nor there."

"I'm sure this is only a mistake," Janella said.

"Oh no, this is not a mistake. Open your eyes, you're a smart woman we have history."

"I don't know you."

"So, you think," Chloe replied as two maids rushed into the room with bags and first aid kits to assist Janella because she was wounded bad. "Enjoy your day," Chloe said as she stepped in front of the three guards watching over her.

"Don't feed her today let her feel the pain I felt," Chloe said before walking off.

***

Southside, Chi-Town

"It's six of y'all niggas on every corner in one-mile ratios it should be no reason why niggas is on the same team killing niggas oversells," Gucci said to eighteen of his workers in the back of one of his trap houses on Clyde Street.

"That nigga Clip started that shit folk but we ain't know Skinny was going to kill him. They were back and forth with stealing each other's fiends," Lil Weezy said speaking on the event that took place last night on the block they hustled on for Gucci.

Clip and Skinny both worked for Gucci and they were all BD gang members under Gucci. Clip hustled a block away from Skinny and since Skinny was fucking his baby mother, he was stealing all his fiends.

Last night Skinny was fed up with Clip's disrespect and approached him which escalated into a heated argument. Not one for arguing, Clip shot Skinny five times killing him on his own block.

The police were parked up the block working undercover watching the whole scene unfold. At first, they weren't going to call it in because both men were two low life street punks. When Clip shot himself in the head, they had no choice but to call it in.

"I don't give a fuck who started it we have to move as a unit as one because we all the same, bro," Gucci said. Everybody nodded in agreement. "Now the block is hot, so everybody take two days off and no killing. I know we got smoke with the Latin Kings but fall back for a couple of days," Gucci said, then walked off, ending his meeting, so he could take his side bitch shopping.

Gucci was thirty years old, short, with long dreads, tattoos all over his face, dark skin, and gold teeth. He was a high-ranking BD, months ago he came home from doing a bid in a Miami prison for getting caught with guns in Dade County. He came back with so many keys from his plug he'd robbed in Miami he was all the way up. When he met Black, they clicked tight and Gucci found a new plug with the best Heroin he'd ever seen.

Gucci was a Heroin dealer and user but he kept his personal life out of the streets. Gucci was named Gucci because he only wore Gucci clothes ever since his younger days.

It was a nice, sunny summer day so everybody was outside running around finding shit to do or on their way to chill under someone AC.

Gucci had a navy-blue Mercedes AMGC63 cape with tints and 20-inch rims. He had a wife named Lily who's a Spanish woman that he met years ago in Miami and ended up moving her to Chicago. She was Cuban and beautiful. Being married didn't stop him from cheating because he had a cute, hoodrat, yellow bitch from K-town whose pussy and head game was to kill for, she was expensive but worth spending a bag on.

Gucci had to re-up tomorrow from Black because he was down half of key and he had six blocks doing big numbers. He was into a beef with the Latin Kings because one of his guys killed a known king outside a club for his chain and Rolex watch. Gucci tried to dead the beef, but the kings weren't having it; they wanted blood, so it was war. Gucci rode around with two Dracos on his passenger seat.

Chapter 4

Buff City

Hitler was up at the break of dawn in a Dunkin Donuts parking lot drinking a cup of Espresso, leaning on his black on black Shelby Super Snake Mustang. Hitler was in love with fast cars and the Shelby and Hellcat he had were hands down speed demands. He checked his Rolex Dayton, 18k White gold, leather strap, and confirmed that his plug was a couple of minutes late.

Hitler was now dealing coke and dope in his hood because the profit was triple what he would make off pills and selling lean. The gang was all eating in Bluff City thanks to Hitler feeding the guys.

Lil BD had been missing for days now. Hitler went to his crib and Jenny was just as lost. She was worried to death about her husband. Hitler figured Lil DB was laying low because of the beef with Chi'Raq Gangstas.

There wasn't a day Hitler didn't think about what they did to his grandma who raised him since he was a baby. Hitler felt as if they were so close to catching the crew, but it was like everybody vanished out of the blue. Regardless the show had to go on and he had to get to a bag to feed his guys.

A silver Nissan GTR sped into the lot while a black Tahoe parked across the street as if it was a hit.

Day-Day hopped out in a red Saint Laurent outfit inhaling the morning warm air.

"Hitler, sorry for the wait," Day-Day said smiling and embracing Hitler.

Hilter gave him a sour look. Hitler didn't really like Day-Day. Not because he was cocky and loud, but because he knew he was a coward. Hitler hated niggas who used money as a shield or a cover-up for who they really are. Growing up the OGs used to always tell Hitler money don't make a real nigga or a man.

"Who them niggas?" Hitler said looking at the SUV parked across the street.

"Those my guys, we about to head out to Ohio real quick, so I'm in a rush. What you got for me? I hope it's all there," Day-Day said.

Hitler was about to spaz on him but he remained cool. "It's all here and everything for the new shipment that I expect to receive tonight," Hitler said as he grabbed a big duffle bag out of the passenger seat and passed it to Day-Day.

"A'ight I got you, I'ma call you," Day-Day said as he placed the money in the Nissan then pulled out of the exit entrance of the lot.

Hitler climbed in his car shaking his head, something about Day-Day rubbed him wrong since it had ever since he'd first met him two weeks ago through a chick he knew. Anytime an opportunity would present itself for Hitler to show the coward what he was really about Hitler was going to take it.

***

Bolingbrook, IL.

Rosie was in the shower washing her hair, letting the hot water relax her body. Since leaving Boss a couple of months ago things had been mentally hard on her because Boss was all she'd known for years. There was no denying he was an amazing husband and lover but what he did she could never see herself forgiving. When she found out Boss killed her brother, she looked at him differently because Boss knew how much she loved Mike.

Being a Latin Queen, she stood tall for her Kings and Queens, so for her to know who killed a King and her own brother was heavy on her heart. There was no denying the fact that she truly missed him, but she had to be strong.

A couple of weeks ago Rosie saw on the local Chicago news a mass killing at Boss' car dealership, but the victims were all Haitian immigrants. Rosie called every jail and hospital looking for Boss, but he was nowhere to be found.

His home was still intact just as it was the same day she'd left. She knew anything could've happened but she prayed he was okay and just on a vacation.

No matter what he did she could never turn her back on the man she loved and cared for. She lived in a nice middle-class neighborhood. Her house had four bedrooms, three bathrooms, and heated floors, brick & stone estate, a spacious living room with a three-sided fireplace, cherry oak wood floors, a private lake, and a private sun deck in the back.

Boss left her a lot of money she had no clue he'd placed in her account the same night she left, he just wanted to assure that she was financially stable.

She climbed out of the shower and placed a Versace robe over her body, then she walked into her private suite fit for a Queen with Mink rugs, a fireplace, a walk-in closet, a private terrace, and a canopy bed.

Rosie turned on her state-of-the-art surround sound system she played her favorite song, *Miss Kissing Ya* by *Tamar Braxton*. Rosie lotioned her sexy tone, perfect body before putting on her Fendi pajamas, and laying down since she had an early day ahead of her.

Tomorrow she planned to open a new salon with a barbershop connected. She still had her Rosie Salon downtown in Chicago but she wasn't ready to go back to the city no time soon, so she let Naja manage the place.

In less than an hour, Rosie was knocked out snoring lightly in her bed with her favorite song on repeat. Rosie woke up out of her sleep, she thought she'd felt a tight grip around her neck. She assumed she was having another bad dream until she saw a large man dressed in all black with a mask over his face choking the life out of her.

Animal had a tight grip crushing her windpipe, and her oxygen levels started to decrease. Rosie tried to get loose but the more she moved the more pressure he put on her neck strangling her to death. Close to four minutes later Rosie's body was completely still and lifeless.

"Bitch," Animal said to himself with a laugh taking one last look at Rosie's body before walking out of her house.

***

Animal was parked in her driveway next to her Lexus acting like he lived there, he drove off in his Nissan Sentra listening to G-Herbo's mixtape, bobbing his head and feeling the real-life Chi'Raq shit the young nigga was spitting on the tracks.

Animal had been stalking Rosie for a couple of days. He even had her whole routine down pat. She was a serious piece of eye candy no wonder Boss kept her a secret. Not even a dummy would bring her around the guys because she would make any trusted friend turn disloyal.

Boss was nowhere to be found or Malik, Animal felt something was up, he thought they were on to him. The night he let Malik get away was his first mistake, something told him to kill him from the jump and then he coulda handle Lil BD and Hitler's ambush.

Chloe was making him a very rich man and he loved her more for that. He was ready to propose to her but he knew she was a different breed so he chose to wait. Animal felt no regret for crossing his guys, he knew it was a way of life, especially in the motherland.

Chapter 5

Port-Au-Prince, Haiti

Boss and Lil BD were in the mansion gym filled with state-of-the-art exercise equipment from bench presses, dumbbells, pull-ups bars, matted floors, mirrors, free-weights, and brand new university machines.

"Damn, bro, you gotta get your weight up," Boss told Lil BD who was having a hard time curling the 90-pound dumbbells.

"I'ma get back into it. What you think Hitler and Malik gonna think about us on the same time now? After everything that happened," Lil BD asked as he stopped walking out.

That question had been on his mind for days because he knew it would be hard to keep Hitler on a leash after the Chi'Raq Gangsters murdered his grandma.

"I only hope they can see the bigger picture, bro. Because regardless we brothers and it's fucked up we have to go through this for us to become as one," Boss stated doing a 30-clip on the pull-up bar.

"Was you really going to kill me?" Lil DB asked seriously.

"Of course," Boss replied.

"Good the feeling was mutual, bro," Lil BD said, both men shared a laugh.

"I wonder what type of training this nigga got for us? If it's some military shit, I'm not wit' it," Lil BD said.

"I don't know but I know it's more mental than physical. I can tell our grandfather is a wise man. So, let's just listen and soak up the game," Boss said.

Luc walked into the gym in a black suit which was his regular attire just like his father. "Gentlemen."

"Luc," Boss said.

"I hate to be the one to deliver this news, Boss. But your wife Rosie was found murdered in her home earlier today, I'm sorry," Luc said.

Boss felt his knees weaken as he took a seat and covered his face trying to hold in his pain and tears.

"I'm sorry, bro," Lil BD said comforting his brother and Luc joined them because he hated to see his family in distress.

"How did she die?" Boss asked with a straight face looking at his uncle.

"She was strangled to death."

"Animal," Boss stated already knowing how he got down.

"I should have been killed that goofy nigga," Lil BD said.

"I want to go to her funeral."

"We can arrange that but you're going to be heavily guarded," Luc stated and Boss nodded.

"I want to go with him," Lil BD said.

"That's not a good idea. I think you should stay back, we have to prepare you," Luc told BD.

"Stay back, BD, I'ma be right back."

"A'ight," Lil BD said, worried about his brother. He started to worry about Jenny's safety now because she knew Animal.

***

Two Weeks Later

Southside, Chi-Town

Rosie's funeral service was being held at Kingdom Graveyard on a scorching hot summer day. Over three hundred Latin Kings and Queens came out to show respect to Rosie, who was well respected and well-liked within the gang.

Everybody wore black and gold colors, some who knew her was crying while others didn't care at all. Most of the people who were there were only there because they had to be, it was part of their gang code to show up at fallen soldiers' funerals.

Latin Kings surrounded the graveyard while the ceremony was going on in Spanish by a Roman Catholic Priest from Puerto Rico.

Boss and six black, tinted SUVs pulled up to the graveyard catching everybody's attention. Boss hopped out of the first truck and five dread heads hopped out behind him from each SUV.

Boss told them to wait inside the SUVs. He was okay.

"You know someone here?" one of the security niggas standing like a soldier with eight kings with him asked.

"I'm Boss, she's my wife." When Boss said that the men cleared the way for him, they all knew who the man was.

"Sorry for your loss," one of the Latin kings said.

Boss slowly nodded and stood in the back watching the ceremony trying to hold his tears, but he couldn't any longer. Tear filled his eyes behind his Gucci shades as people eyed him wondering who he was.

Once the graveyard cleared, Boss went to pay his respects and talk to his deceased wife. After two hours of crying and releasing his deep emotions, he was ready to leave but first, he had to make one stop to drop off a note.

***

Downtown, Chi-Town

Malik sat in the upper class, four-star restaurant that recently opened waiting for his guest to arrive, so he could speak to her to figure some shit out. The past couple of weeks Malik had been hiding out in his condo because there was a lot of fishy shit going on and he wanted to sit back and observe everything.

When he saw what happened to Boss' car dealership on the news, he thought it was a Fed bust, until he saw the victims were all immigrants. Boss was nowhere to be found which made him worry.

After he saw the news of Rosie there was no doubt in his mind that someone could have killed Boss also.

This was Malik's first time out of his crib in months and he was ready for any type of confrontation with twin Desert Eagles on his waist.

Malik reached out to the only survivor, Boss' assistant Kylie. When he told her he was Boss's best friend she didn't believe him until he told her his government name. Kylie remembered Boss telling her his boy Malik was coming home and he wanted her to order him the new white Maybach.

Waiting in the far back Malik saw a sexy, white woman in a black dress with pumps on her manicured toes and blonde long hair.

"Malik?" Kylie said in a soft voice while taking off her shades showing her sexy blue eyes.

"Yes, sit please," Malik said standing up and pulling her chair out, shocking her.

"Thank you." Kylie looked at him thinking how handsome he was.

"Are you okay? You look a little nervous," he said.

"Of course, I am you, asshole," she replied with an attitude.

"Sorry didn't mean to offend you but what happened that night?"

"I was working late as always then I saw a gang of men running into the car dealership on the cameras. I yelled to tell Boss but then I felt something shoot me in my neck. I thought I was dying but I got dizzy. I heard gunshots coming from Boss's office. I passed out and the next thing I knew I was in a hospital. The hospital people told me I was sleep for two days straight," Kylie informed me.

"They shot you with a tranquilizer?" Malik asked suspiciously, never hearing no shit like that. He started to wonder if she was lying. "Do you think Boss made it out alive?" he asked.

"I don't know, I hope so. I would've given my life for him," she said.

"I'ma figure this shit out, but if you need anything or remember anything call me. I'm sorry you had to experience this. I'm here for you," he said looking into her sexy eyes feeling a connection.

"Okay, nice meeting you, Malik," Kylie said as she got up to leave.

Malik watched her curvy frame swing and stared at her nice ass swaying as if she had no panties on. Kylie had been doing squats and exercising to get a bigger ass because she was tired of her flat ass.

Malik left with many new concerns on his mind that didn't add up. It was like a puzzle with missing pieces.

Romell Tukes

Chapter 6

Robins, IL

Malik made it back home to his condo to see a letter in his mailbox. It was Sunday, he knew the mailman only worked Monday through Saturday, so he was lost to who'd left it in his mailbox. Entering his home, he took off his shoes so he could keep his white, thick carpet clean that he'd paid a lot of cash for. Sitting down in his living room he opened the letter and began reading it,

Malik, bro, I'm sorry for the wait. I know you been worried about me but I'm safe. I'm in Haiti, I was kidnapped by my grandfather who runs the Haitian Cartel or Mafia whatever this shit is lol. Me and Lil' BD down here, we all on the same time now. My mom was kidnapped by the Columbia Cartel. Guess who runs the Cartel? The wife of the detective we killed and she's fucking Animal. Bro, listen close Animal been playing us, he is Black and he killed Rosie. Soon I'll be in Miami, I'ma need you down there with me so be ready. Stay safe and keep your eyes open. I love you, bro.
Boss

Malik couldn't believe what he read. The letter answered all his questions. The news about Animal didn't shock him. He always felt he was the disloyal type, but Boss always gave people the benefit of the doubt. After the night Animal tried to kill him, he vowed to kill Animal wherever he caught him at.

Malik sent Kylie a text letting her know her boss was okay. Seconds later, she texted back. *//: OMG, I'm so happy. Thank you! Hope to see you soon again.*

Malik was about to text back some slick shit until a vision of Simone popped in his head. He could never let Simone's emotions go; she had his heart and soul but he knew he had to move to let some of the pain of her death go or he would only relive it daily.

***

Comendador, DR

"Mmmm! Oohhh, yesss, luuuu!" Lela screamed out while rolling her hips into Luc's hard thrusts. Luc was fucking Lela on her side raising her thick left leg getting deep in her tight moist waterfall. "Oooohhh shit, papi" she yelled while grabbing a pillow.

Luc was tearing her ass up giving his wife deep sensual strokes. "Talk that shit now," Luc said pulling her hair pumping in and out of her sex muscles, bouncing on her big ass.

Pleaseeee—fuck me—harderrrr," she cried out as he slipped a thumb in her tiny brown hole. "I'm cumming!" she screamed as her lower body jerked while catching an orgasm.

Luc turned her over on all fours seeing her phat pussy poke out *like a juicy peach with no fur.* Luc's dick was coated with her creamy cum. Lela's pussy was mind-blowing and a God's gift of life the way it gripped his dick with care and power.

His dick parted her pussy lips, sliding inside of her, digging in her core.

"Fuck this dick," he said in his masculine voice.

Lela's ass was so big and wide it was hard for her to take dick inside her tight pussy, but she did her best.

"Don't hurt me, papi," she moaned burying her head into the pillow. Luc spanked her ass making it clap. "Ugghhh, uhhmmm shh," she grunted while he controlled her small waist movements fucking the soul out of her until they both reached their peak.

"You need to come out here more. Your kids miss you and me," Lela said lying in bed in her strong Spanish accent.

Lela was breathtaking, she was Dominican, light-skinned, medium-height, with almond eyes, thin, perfect eyebrows, thick lips, naturally long eyelashes, high cheekbones, dimples, and perfect jaw structure. She had her titties and ass done twice by the best doctors in DR, her measurements were 36-28-46 she was stacked up.

"I'm sorry, love, things been crazy in Haiti while preparing my nephews."

"How are they?" Lela asked in bad English, smoking a cigarette and watching her husband get dressed.

Luc and Lela had been married for ten years with two daughters ages six and eight.

"They're okay. They have a lot of potential."

"Good, my father wants to have a sit down with you sometime next month. I told him you'll be there," Lela said giving him a look letting him know that he'd better be there.

Lela's father was the biggest drug supplier in DR, and he was a powerful drug lord.

"I'll be there, I'm taking the girls out. You coming?" Luc asked seeing how tired she looked.

"Oh, no I need a break. You enjoy yourself, babe," she said getting under her satin covers to fall asleep.

Luc went to wake his beautiful little girls up to take them out for a whole day of fun.

***

Golden Beach, FL

The Santos Cartel was Columbia's biggest Cartel family run by Hector and his underboss Mark.

Hector was born and raised in Pereira, Colombia in a rough time during the conflict between government forces, anti government insurgent groups, and Cartel families. Hector climbed his way to the top of the food chain with no help.

He had a big family but years ago his wife was killed along with his son and sister during a drug war. Hector sold tons of coke, Heroin, Ecstasy, and weapons, so he was a big name in the underground world.

Since a kid, he'd always wanted a house on the beach and now he had the biggest house in the Golden Beach area, which was surrounded by millionaires. Hector's mansion was 21,619 square feet, with fourteen rooms, ten bathrooms, a safe room, three-floor levels, a private elevator, a foyer, a library, walls of glass, two pools, and a wet bar with granite countertops. It was also equipped with a ten car garage and an expensive line up of luxury cars parked in the wrap-around driveway.

Hector was in his movie theater watching his favorite movie of all time, *Scarface,* he knew word for word. At age 50 he took good care of himself by eating healthy, exercising, meditating, and staying very active. He was 5'10, 170 pounds, had a bald head, a clean-cut face, glasses, tan skin, and a lean build.

In less than an hour, he had to fly out to Columbia to meet with Mark about Chloe. He hated Chloe with a passion, he'd tried to kill her many times, but it was like she always expected death.

He heard she was back in Miami dealing with the Pero Cartel, a family he'd never dealt with but knew of. Chloe had something up her sleeve and Hector wasn't going to sit back and let her plans unfold before his eyes.

"Hector, your daughter is calling," one of his guards said walking into the movie theater with Hector's phone.

All Hector's men knew not to interrupt him while he watched Scarface unless it was a serious emergency or his beautiful daughter called, who was in college most of the time at the University of Miami.

After talking to his daughter for thirty minutes the movie was over, so it was time for him to leave. He left on his private jet he owned with twenty of his goons.

Chapter 7

Port-Au Prince, Haiti

Francisque and Luc stood watching Boss and Lil' BD sprint back and forth in the field.

"How they coming along?" Francisque asked.

"Good to my surprise," Luc stated, watching the two men sprint for forty-five minutes straight with no breaks.

"You think they're ready for their first mission?"

"I hope so, but I have a little plan for the Gutierrez Family. First, I plan to send them at Manuel the copo," Luc said as he checked his watch and blew his whistle for Boss and Lil' BD to step.

"I hear he's a party boy but what about Nueva Castro Gutierrez?" Francisque said knowing the boss man wouldn't take the death of his son and copo lightly.

"That's where your plan comes into play, pops. Now I have to finish training. I have a special assignment today." Luc walked toward Boss and Lil BD who was drained.

Francisque walked back to the palace to get some sleep he'd just flown back in from Chile after a meeting.

"Where grandpop going?" Boss asked, seeing his grandfather walk down the road leading to the house.

"Most likely a nap, he always gets jet lag and grumpy," Luc said walking to the barn where his men awaited him.

"What's next? We been training since four a.m., it's one p.m. I'm starving and tired," Lil BD said sweating like an African slave in a cotton field eighty years ago.

Lil BD and Boss wore army uniforms, combat boots, fifty weight vests, and heavy ten-pound ankle weights.

"You will be okay? You have to learn discipline. You may one day be in a situation where you're held captive and you could starve to death. Your heart controls your mind and your mind controls your physical body," Luc stated seriously before they walked into the barn full of goons. "Now since you both are a part of the Haitian Mafia you have to put in a little more work."

"I thought it was the Haitian Cartel?" Lil BD asked.

Laughs filled the room as Luc shook his head

"No, my friend we move like the black John Gotti," Luc said as they walked over to four Haitian's tied in chairs by their ankles and hands, and their mouths were covered with layers of thick rope.

"What's this about?" Boss said, looking at the main, older woman in her seventies, a middle dark-skinned woman, and a little girl no older than nine all tied up in separate chairs.

Boss saw the fear and tears in all their eyes.

"These are about to be part of Lil BD's training for the day. You see Boss I've seen a lot of your work. I was impressed, you showed no fear whatsoever, but your brother has shown me a lot of hesitation many times. This is no place for hesitation, one stagger and you could lose your life at any second," Luc said as Lil BD's face lit up with rage.

"I put in work," Lil BD said.

"I know but it's a difference between putting in work and being cold-hearted," Luc said, passing him a Glock.

Lil BD looked at Boss who gave him a head nod.

Boc! Boc! Boc! Boc! Boc! Boc! Boc! Boc!

Lil BD shot all of them in the forehead twice without blinking before passing the gun back to Luc, showing no type of emotions.

"Good job no question or fear. I thought my gun handle was going to be sweaty. A lot of people get nervous when it comes to kids or elders," Luc said as his goons dragged the dead bodies into the tool area to chop the bodies up into pieces.

"What did they do anyway?" Lil BD asked.

"Nothing," Luc stated as they all left to prepare for some more training.

***

Mexico City, Mexico

Manuel and eight of his guards boarded his Yacht with ten beautiful Mexican women in bikinis ready to have fun. It was a beautiful day for a nice tan and cruise on a Yacht. Manuel was the son of Nueva the Mexican Cartel boss. He was twenty-four years old handsome, wealthy, and very smart just like his father.

Since a teenager, Manuel loved to party and be around beautiful women who wanted to have a great time. He didn't do drugs or drink, he thought it was a weakness but he supplied it to women around him.

"Papi, I want to be the first to suck your dick," a cute, young-looking Mexican chick said with big titties busting out of her bra.

"It's enough to go around. Come on let's go to the upper deck," Manuel said and all the women followed him onto a large deck full of glass tables, chairs, and two stripper poles.

His guards were posted up downstairs and upstairs. The 286ft Yacht glided down the river for a night of fun.

"You two get on the pole and dance," Manuel stated as the rest of the women sniffed coke and Heroin off the glass table.

Two women started dancing for Manuel and taking their clothes off, getting him aroused. The young chick from earlier with the thin lips saw his dick growing in his pants and reached for his cock. Within seconds she was deep throating him, giving him sloppy head with no hands.

"Mmmm," Manuel moaned as two other women joined in to help.

***

"You ready, nigga?" Boss asked Lil BD who was next to him under the bar holding onto the bottom cabinet where liquor was normally held.

"Yeah, but hold on, my leg went to sleep," Lil BD said, trying to move his numb legs.

"It's two outside the door, I hear him. Make sure you got your silencer attached to your Draco."

"Roger that, I'm ready," Lil BD said, opening the cabinet doors and climbing out with Boss behind him both dressed in all black, with vests, and extra arsenal strapped all over their bodies as if they were about to go to war.

"Shhh," Boss said as the two guards standing outside the door talked.

Boss told Lil BD to get on the wall beside the door. Boss saw a heel lying on the floor, he picked it up and tossed it at the door getting their attention.

Psst! Psst! Psst! Psst! Psst! Psst!

Lil BD and Boss tagged- team, killing both Mexicans.

Boss made his way into the hallway with his AR-15 trained in front of him ready to shoot anything in sight.

"In here," Lil BD said pointing at a room where he heard loud moaning. Boss busted in the room to see two guards fucking two Mexican women from the back. Boss and Lil BD riddled their bodies with bullets leaving the Mexicans dicks stuck in the women as they collapsed on the couch.

Boss saw four guards rushing down the hallway so they could fuck the two bitches that their boss gave them to share.

"Aye wait for them all to come in," Boss told his Little brother who was waiting on the door to open so he could let his Draco sound off

All four guards rushed in the room undoing their clothes so they could get to business, bust a nut, and get back to work. When they saw the dead bodies, they all reached for their weapons, but they were too slow. Boss and Lil BD sprayed them with rounds chopping their bodies down.

"The upper deck," Lil BD said as they made their way upstairs.

Hours ago, Boss and Lil BD sneaked on Manuel's Yacht which was very easy. Luc knew Manuel boarded his Yacht every Friday evening to spend time with hookers and any women who were willing to fuck. Upstairs they saw the Yacht's captain steering the Yacht with a Mexican chick giving him a blow job

Psst! Psst! Psst!

Lil BD killed both of them.

"Next level," Boss said, hearing loud music.

On the upper-level Boss saw Manuel fucking one bitch missionary with her legs in the air on a glass table. Another chick was eating his ass.

"Ohhh yesss, fuck me!" the woman screamed before a bullet entered her skull.

Boss and Lil BD took out all the women with ease. Manuel stood there ass nake with a shocked expression. Before he tried to jump into the ocean, Lil BD's Draco bullets tore his back out the frame, hitting Manuel twenty-one times before his body fell into the ocean.

Chapter 8

Southside, Chi-Town

Days Later

Hitler left one of his stash houses on his way to a party across town an all-white affair. A couple of his guys were already in the club waiting on him. It was 11:48 p.m. and the party was over at 1:00 a.m. because Chicago made it a law to shut all clubs down at one o'clock due to the murders and violence that happens after parties.

Hitler climbed in his Benz truck that he'd rented for the weekend because he'd recently crashed his car into a light pole drunk off the lean. Once inside his truck, he pushed the push to start button.

"Don't pull off," Lil BD said, popping up from the back seat scaring the shit out of Hitler.

"Yo', what the fuck, BD?"

"My bad bro but I know you been worried. Shit's been crazy. A nigga got snatched up and woke up in Haiti, bro."

"Damn, I was sick. Me and the guys was ready to turn the city up," Hitler replied.

"Me and my brother are going to be in Miami for a while soon. A cartel family kidnapped our mom," Lil BD said, catching the awkward expression look on his homie's face. "Yeah, that beef shit is dead. We have to get our mom back. It's a bigger picture and I need you out there with me. You're my right hand," Lil BD continued while Hitler sat deep in thought staring out into the dark streets.

"BD them niggas is ops. They killed my grandma. She was all I had, bro. Ain't a day that goes by that I don't shed a tear for her loss."

"I understand that, and I feel your pain, but can you at least do it for me. This nigga Animal is out here supplying the city and he goes by the name Black. He just killed Boss's wife. He is a real enemy, bro, not Boss."

"They all one in my book, bro. I can't believe you're crossing me like this, Joe? I know that's your blood but that never stopped

43

him from putting the wolves on us," Hitler said. "I can't ride with you if you riding with the ops."

"It's like that?" Lil BD asked with a frustrated look.

"Straight like that. Get the fuck out of my truck," Hitler demanded looking into his rearview mirror, locking eyes with his ex-friend.

Lil BD hopped out and watched Hitler pull off in enraged, speeding down the street and running stop signs.

***

The Next Day

Hitler was waiting in his Benz truck for Day Day to arrive in the Lincoln Mall parking lot. There was 325,000 in the backseat for his plug. He hated to ride dirty with a gun and a large amount of money, but he trusted nobody else. The only nigga he trusted had just turned into an op on him which hurt him because he loved Lil BD like a brother.

Hitler was so upset with Lil BD last night, he didn't even make it to the party, he went straight home. Not in a million years would he have seen Lil BD working with Boss especially after everything they'd just gone through in the past year.

When Lil BD told him about his mom, he felt his pain but that was no excuse to cross him for the ops.

A Nissan GTR pulled up next to him honking his horn. Hitler grabbed the duffle bag and hopped out feeling that early summer heat. The mall parking lot was filled with parked cars as people shopped early in the morning to beat the evening weekend rush.

"What's good, big homie?" Day-Day said as Hitler climbed into the small Nissan.

"Ain't shit, here go your three-twenty-four K. I had my guys drop off that one-seventy-five the other day to your people in the Village."

"I got that, bro, gratitude," Day-Day said, placing the money in his backseat.

44

"You know a nigga named, Black? My people have been doing business for years with him. They say he's good people, but I don't know him."

"Yeah, Big Black's my plug. He's big-time, he shows love to me and Gucci," Day-Day said.

"Down South, Gucci?"

"Yeah, but he from Chi'Raq," Day-Day said, wondering why he was asking so many questions.

"I'ma check you later, I'm on my way to Iowa. I got the dog food out there moving," Hilter said getting out of his car.

"A'ight be easy, Joe," Day-Day said, pulling off.

Hitler planned to pay Gucci a visit, he knew a little bitch that he was fucking in his hood and he had one person on his mind Animal.

***

Downtown, Chi-Town

Jenny returned from food shopping and looking for a job because she had too much free time on her hands.

Ever since the night Lil BD left her, she'd been emotionally disturbed and losing sleep. After Lil BD told her Boss was her brother, she couldn't forget the night she shot him. She could only imagine how he felt about her. She'd even been trying to find him, but it was as if he'd vanished just like BD.

She walked into her bedroom to see white roses on her bed. Jenny grabbed the roses and searched her condo as tears rolled down her beautiful face ruining her makeup.

Lil BD was the only person on earth that knew she loved white roses and how much it meant to her. She could smell Lil BD's savory aroma.

Jenny saw no letter, no traces, nothing but she could feel his presence was there. She knew he was alive which brought a smile to her face, but her heart missed him, and she needed to be back in his arms.

***

Southside, Chi-Town

Gucci was in Tammy's apartment on 122nd and State Street sitting on her dirty couch, watching roaches race back and forth on her living room table.

"Babe, you almost ready?" Tammy yelled from her backroom while she got ready for her job at the upscale strip club Sky II downtown next door to City Hall and the parole building.

"I'm waiting on you. Who is going to look after your kids?" Gucci said as Tammy came out of her room in a purple and white net dress with thongs and a bra under.

Her hair was dyed blue and her body was thick and wide with no stomach. She was dark-skinned and full-blooded Jamaican. Her sex game was crazy, but only big spenders could get a taste of her.

Tammy had three kids with three different baby fathers. All of them were in prison now and she didn't do shit for any of them, not even send pictures of their kids.

"Nigga, Chris is twelve-years-old he can watch over his little brothers. He's almost a grown man," she said putting on her heels.

"If you say so."

"How was it tonight, baby? You got my fucking asshole hurting," she said jumping in his lap.

"I had better but you'll do," Gucci said, making her get up with an attitude.

He watched her wide ass wobble and bounce every time her foot hit the ground. In the club, her name was Earthquake because she didn't have to do much to make her ass move like an earthquake.

"How much you got for me?" she said seriously.

Gucci pulled out a wad of money and slammed it on the table killing a gang of roaches.

"I have to go, come on," Gucci said, getting up, dusting dog fur off his Gucci outfit. "Since when you get a dog?"

"I don't the couch just a little old," Tammy said walking out of her apartment. "The club should be poppin', right now. You staying to trick on me?"

"I've done enough of that," Gucci said seeing a nigga with a hoodie pop out from the side alley of her crib. Gucci saw a shiny chrome gun in the man's hand when he came into the light. "Duck!" Gucci yelled, pulling out his 9mm.

Boom! Boom! Boom! Boom! Boom! Boom! Boom! Boom!

Hitler left Gucci and Tammy slumped on her building stairs.

A group of teens was out there chilling until they heard the shots and they hauled ass off the block.

Hitler hopped in his Benz truck burning rubber. He saw a couple of faces he knew ducking hopping the gunfire was clear. Hitler knew Tammy well she was his cousin, but she was a shady bitch and he'd never liked her. So, killing two birds with one gun made it easy for him.

Romell Tukes

Chapter 9

Verrettes, Haiti

Boss and Lil BD held MP assault rifles in a shooting range.

"Shoot!" Luc screamed.

Boss and Lil BD squeezed the trigger shooting at the paper targets fifty yards away.

"Stop! Go get targets," Luc told one of his men rushing to grab the 22nd target sheet.

Luc used this gun range to train his men so they could be ready for war at any time. Luc looked at the large paper with holes directly in the middle of the target's bullseye on both papers.

"Wow, you both are accurate shooters. Now let's see if you can do one-hundred yards? Bring them in!" Luc yelled.

Two niggas with pillowcases over their heads were brought into the worn-down warehouse.

"Take both of them to the end," Luc instructed.

"Let me guess what he did J walked?" Lil BD said sarcastically.

"We don't have Jaywalking out here, but we do have rapists. These two gentlemen raped two nine-year-old little girls. In Haiti we don't tolerate that kind of disgrace," Luc said with a stern look on his face.

Boss shook his head and aimed his MP 100 yards away trying to get a good shot.

"Take off the shit on his face!" Boss yelled to the goons standing on the sideline watching. When they took the pillowcases off the rapist's heads both men were crying and making ugly faces.

"Good," Boss said as he lined up the shot and took it.

The bullet ripped through one of the men's skulls with only one shot. Lil BD saw the body drop and was impress glad he didn't get into a gun battle with his big brother.

"Lil BD your turn. One shot, you miss you come train in the mountains," Luc said looking at Lil BD roll his eyes. Luc was extra hard on Lil BD because he had a lot of potential, he just needed a strong push.

Lil BD picked up the weapon aiming it at the next victim. After lining up the shot Lil BD took it, he only missed his target by a few inches.

"Fuck!" Lil BD shouted.

"Put it down. I want you to listen. Any time you shoot, never focus too much on your target, try to focus on your weapon and distance. Relax your mind and body. Never shoot in a rush, time your time and your target will come to you," Luc said, handing Lil BD the MP while the rapist screamed something out in Creole.

Lil BD relaxed his body and focused on his weapon while lining up the distance and the target then firing, hitting the target in the middle of his forehead.

"Good job, bro," Boss said.

"Good, but you still got training in the mountains," Luc said, walking off.

"What?" Lil BD said not trying to train in the mountains again because the other night he almost got bitten by a snake and attacked by a tiger.

"I'll go with you scared nigga," Boss said laughing as they followed Luc and his goons.

***

Miami Beach, FL

Victor of the Peru Cartel was waiting in his office for Chloe to come upstairs, she'd just arrived for their meeting.

Since Victor started supplying Chloe Heroin she'd made him millions in a short duration of time. She was the ideal business partner but lately, her name had been in the mix of some big shit and he called her to see what the fuck was going on.

Victor tried his best not to mix business with pleasure or violence because that was a mix of failure, and failing wasn't in his goals.

Chloe walked into his office in a nice white, satin Celine slit dress and heels.

"Victor, how are you, love?" Chloe said sitting down in his Brazilian oak chair that matched his Brazilian oak hardwood floors.

"I'm good. Thanks for coming out. I had no clue you were in the area."

"I got a home a few blocks away from you Victor. This area is amazing, seventeen point nine million dollars is well worth every penny for my estate," she said.

"Great, how's business?"

"Thanks to you I'm expanding throughout the Midwest. I'm waiting on the new shipment. That's why you called me here correct? Because I'm sure a busy man such as yourself has better things to do than just waste time looking at me."

"I paused the shipment until further notice."

"Why?" she said with anger raising.

"Your name is into some serious shit. I want to know what's going on. We've been straightforward since I've met you, so I don't want to be left in the blind," he said looking at her puzzled facial expression.

Victor stared at her confused look thinking about how well she played the game.

"Victor, I honestly have no fucking clue what you're talking about."

"The Mexican Cartel from Mexico City?"

"Nuevo and Manuel?" she replied.

"Si."

Chloe knew who they were because they had a big dope line from Mexico to Texas that supplied the West coast and certain parts of the south.

"I don't deal with them, so I don't know what issue they could have with me."

"They're saying you killed Manuel on his boat with eighteen others," he said looking into her eyes for any truth.

"What! Me? Victor, that's not possible I've been in Colombia for weeks. I came to Miami two days ago," she said.

"I don't know but they received a dozen roses with your signature on it saying let the games begin," Victor said repeating the information he heard from another Mexican Family.

"Victor, I swear someone is trying to set me up. It's the oldest trick in the book. You have to believe me."

"Well, the oldest trick in the book got you in a ton of shit because they want you dead. I'm willing to help as much as possible but the shipment will be on hold until we take care of this issue," he said.

Chloe nodded her head and made her way out of his place of business.

Chapter 10

Downtown, Chi-Town

Hitler was parked in his Benz SUV at a fancy five-star hotel. Waiting on Day Day to come out from his night stay with a sexy dark-skinned chick that he'd left the club with.

It was 8:00 a.m. and summertime was starting to break into the fall season. The city was saddened about the loss of Gucci because he was looking out for a lot of niggas in the hood where he lived.

The streets assumed the Latin Kings killed him because of the crazy beef the two crews had going on. A lot of people said Hitler did the hit himself but everybody knew Hitler, so giving him up wasn't happening, plus they refused to end up like Gucci and Tammy.

Since his visit from BD, his mind was blurry. He was only focused on finding Animal, then he had plans to go to Miami. He made a decision to go look for Boss himself and if Lil BD got in his way he had plans for him too.

Hitler was tired and weak from staying up all night staring at the entrance of the hotel looking for Day Day. His eyes were burning, his neck was stiff, and his lower back pain was driving him crazy and making him uncomfortable in his seat.

Looking at his iPhone he saw a text from Cara a nurse he'd recently met at a Starbucks coffee shop downtown.

//: *Good Morning.* The text read.

His life had been so busy lately he hadn't had time for himself or pussy but after he took care of Day Day, he planned to make time.

Watching Day Day and a dark-skinned chick walk out of the hotel doors brought joy to his morning.

***

Day-Day spent all night fucking the shit out of Raven in the most expensive hotel in Chicago, but Raven was well worth the price.

Raven was a short, petite, cute African chick with the biggest pussy Day Day had ever laid eyes on.

"When can I see you again, zaddy?" Raven said blocking the morning sun from her eyes as they walked to Day Day's car.

"Whenever your pussy heals from the beat down, I just put on it."

"I can't even walk straight," Raven said, walking on her toes.

Day Day climbed inside his car not even opening the door for Raven but last night he did every time she got in and out of his car. Now that he'd already fucked, he planned to treat her like any other bitch.

"Damn, you're not a gentleman no more, I see," she said opening the door for herself.

Boc! Boc! Boc! Boc! Boc! Boc!

Raven's body fell into his car with bullets in her chest ending her life.

Day Day was starting his car until he felt four bullets bang into his upper chest.

"Ahhh!" Day Day screamed.

Hitler grabbed him out of the car. "Where is Black?"

"I don't know, I just know he lives in a condo on Lakeshore Drive. Please I'm just a drug dealer," Day-Day said needing medical attention.

Boc! Boc!

Hitler fired two shots in his head before walking off.

***

Bagota, Columbia

Janella was watching the old fashion TV in front of her bed while two guards sat in chairs outside of her door. Janella couldn't speak Spanish so she couldn't understand what was going on in the news.

There was a lot of killing in Bogota and drug wars. That was all she saw on the news, but she had no clue it was all Chloe's people warring against the Colombia government.

Janella was starting to get used to this crazy lifestyle. The only thing that worried her was her family and their whereabouts. She knew if her father got wind of this, he would eventually have an army at Chloe's doorsteps to get his daughter back.

Being raised in the Haitian Mafia was rough. She was traumatized by everything she saw growing up as a kid. Her father used to make her, and her brothers watch him murder people so they could have cold veins and a heart of steel.

When she came to the states, she saw a different way of living and human beings. Haiti was cold but Chicago was full of good-hearted people with love for each other lives, unlike Haiti.

The lifestyle her father lived, she never wanted that type of energy around her kids, so she kept him a secret and distant for their sake.

Janella had to find a way out of here, she had no clue who Chloe was, she'd never seen her a day in her life.

A guard brought her a TV dinner with a plastic fork and a bottle of water.

"Thank you," she said with puppy dog eyes as the man spit in her food before walking off, laughing.

Janella saw the gob of spit in the mashed potatoes, she just ate the gravy and steak. After closing her eyes, she went to sleep dreaming of better days.

***

Next Door

Chloe was in her master bedroom suite, fresh out of the shower from her trip from Miami Beach. She wore a long white T-shirt with heels.

The news of her beef with Nueva was new to her and shocking but she refused to let Nueva or any Cartel Family ax her out of the picture, she'd come too far in life.

"Chloe, you in there?" RJ said knocking on his sister's French double doors.

"Yeah," she answered.

"What's the emergency? I was at home with the family about to go out to the beach," RJ said, sitting on her bed as she looked at herself in the mirror placing her long hair in a ponytail.

"We have a bigger problem, RJ. We're at war with the Mexican Cartel."

"How? That doesn't make sense. What family is it?" he stated nervously because he knew the Mexican Cartel families were nothing to fuck with.

"Nueva and his people. They think I killed his son Manuel," Chloe said sitting next to him.

"Did you?" he asked knowing his sister was very grimy.

"No, I didn't, RJ. Someone is setting me up but we have to come up with something."

"We? Chloe, you better use your puppet Animal. I got shit going on."

"RJ you're the capo and my brother, so when they come you will be first if we don't strike first. I have a plan so don't worry. Okay," she said rubbing his hand then placing it on her juicy thick thigh.

"I be thinking about the time I sucked your dick. I would love for you to return the favor," Chloe said sexily, cocking her legs open while placing his hand on her phat pussy.

When RJ felt she had no panties on he was turned on especially feeling her smooth bald pussy. RJ placed a finger in her wetness feeling her walls squeeze his finger

"Mmmm," she moaned in a sexy voice as she took off her shirt exposing her titties

"Eat me," she said while RJ buried his face in her pussy tasting her opening. RJ flicked his tongue in and out her slit to taste her sweet juices.

"Yessss, RJJJJ," she moaned.

RJ parted her thin pussy lips with his tongue as if he was French kissing her clit. He palmed her ass while she rode his mouth.

"Ohhh, ple-ple-ple-pleaseee!"

RJ focused on sucking her clit and fingering her pussy at the same time.

"I'm cumming," she cried out.

RJ made his long, pointed tongue dance inside her love box until she came all over his face. RJ saw her cum pouring down into her asshole. He lifted her ass, then turned her over and started licking her ass. His tongue traced around her tiny brown hole as she arched her back so his tongue could get deeper.

"Oh, my God!" she screamed, grabbing her pillow looking back at him. RJ spread her ass cheeks and ate her ass like he hadn't eaten in years.

Chloe came twice before he stopped with a hard-on. "Come here," she said pulling out his dick, slowly sucking it, and looking him in his eyes while he stood up

"Uhmmm," he moaned while she went deep wrapping her lips around his dick and sucking him off until she felt his warm juices burst into her mouth before swallowing every drop.

"I'll handle Nueva," RJ said, pulling up his pants, unable to walk.

"I can't wait until I give you all of me," she said kissing his lips.

Chapter 11

Downtown, Chi-Town

Malik was sitting outside of a new soul food restaurant he'd been waiting to eat at for a while now. It was a nice fall day so eating outside was perfect for the weather.

The past couple of weeks Malik had been trying to hunt down Animal to only come up short every time. He was awaiting Kylie this would be their second time meeting. They would text here and there but nothing serious. There was no denying the chemistry they shared but there was something holding them back.

Kylie was walking through the small restaurant full of black people trying to beat the lunch hour rush.

"Hello," she said approaching him from behind.

"Hey, Kylie, thanks for coming out. Let me get that chair for you," Malik said, pulling out her seat while looking at her toned body in her work-out MGG *Muscle Gang Gear*.

"I was in the gym up the street when you text me," Kylie said, putting her hair in a ponytail.

"I see but Boss left a letter at my crib, he's well. I plan to go to Miami soon to pay him a visit. I just wanted to tell you in person," Malik said

"You told me this in a text," she recalled as a waiter came out to take their order.

"Yeah, but I just thought it would be better in person," he said, and she gave him a funny look.

"I'm glad he's safe. Since they closed his car dealership, I found another state job, so I've been working hard," she said.

"What do you do?"

"I do files for the county police. I hate being around police all day especially in Will county."

"It's better than Cook county."

"Oh, my God you have no clue."

"You're very beautiful, Kylie," Malik said as she looked at him and grabbed her purse to leave. "Kylie, wait. No disrespect," Malik said, grabbing her hands softly.

"What type of games are you trying to play, Malik?"

"I've just been thinking about you since I laid eyes on you and I like you. I want to get to know you, Kylie."

"Malik, you're out of my league. I think you're sniffing up on the wrong dog. Maybe you should find one of these Instagram models, they're more your speed," she said seriously.

The waiter came with two dishes of fried chicken, greens, fried Whiting fish, and homemade cornbread.

"I don't want them, Kylie. They're not my type, I know what I want."

"You don't know nothing about me. I could have been a crack whore," she said, looking into his eyes and seeing that he wasn't breaking.

"I don't care about that. I care about what I see in you today."

"Oh, yeah, well let me give you a little history about me, Mr. Malik," she said leaning into the table showing her cleavage. "When Boss met me, I was working for his Uncle Jay. I was his bottom whore until Carolina came around."

"Hold on, Carolina the cop chick?"

"Yeah. How you know her?"

"I was framed for her murder."

"Oh, shit that was you? I saw you all over the news for the other cop, too," she said.

"Yeah."

"Well, I was a drug addict and whore until Boss sent me to rehab and got me a job at the car dealership. I got my life together. I may look perfect but I'm not. I see you still here," she said eating her fish.

"I can never judge a person for their flaws or mistakes. I'm not perfect I live a dangerous life and I did a lot of horrible things to people, but that doesn't change who I am does it?" he asked her.

"No, not in my books."

"Can I get to know you more?"

"Maybe, but first we gotta order some more of this chicken." She laughed. I'm a white girl but I know some good chicken when I taste it," she said before Malik ordered them more food. The evening went by smoothly, they planned to have a real date soon.

***

Jacmel, Haiti

Luc, Boss, Lil BD, and thirty Haitian shooters were all on the large boat on their way to Trinidad.

"This is a big mission because most likely your targets will shoot back. This is the blueprint of the mansion," Luc said laying out a GPS into Hochoy's crib. "We will take the Pitch Lake directly into his backyard because he normally keeps six guards in the front and over twenty guards inside," Luc said looking at his nephews.

"Who is this nigga?" Lil BD asked with black paint on his face to match his black attire.

"Hochoy used to work for our family until he got as you Americans say *big-headed*. He started to deal with the Trinidad Mafia, our rivals," Luc said.

"You know this nigga's whole layout," Boss said looking at the blueprint studying every part of the house.

"I have two inside workers in his circle. The lights are going to be shut off, so make sure you use your night vision goggles, or you're just as good as dead. This is your last phase of training before you both head out to Miami," Luc said.

"Which way are we going inside?" Lil BD asked.

"That's where shit gets tricky because there is only one way in without causing a scene and that his bedroom balcony."

"And how the fuck do you think we're supposed to get up there?" Boss asked.

"The rope with the hook will lock onto his rail if you throw it correctly as you were both taught," Luc said.

"A'ight, I'm ready. How many of us are going in? We have enough guards," Lil BD stated.

"Oh, no nephew, my men not going in there. We're waiting outside for you and Boss."

"You can't be serious," Lil BD said while Luc passed them two fully loaded RPG assault rifles.

"We're here, come on," Luc said seeing Hochoy's mansion a short distance away.

It was pitch black on the Pitch Lake and hard for Boss to see what was ahead of him.

"You good?" Boss asked his brother.

"Facts, bro, but I have to tell you something if we make it up out of here," Lil BD said.

"We will just focus, bro. Act like we were in the land, drill everything you see in them goggles," Boss stated, seeing the boat pull up to a long walkway.

***

Point Fartin, Trinidad

Hochoy was a drug Lord with strong connections all-across the Caribbean area. He grew up in Haiti at a dangerous time when the police and government robbed and killed the poor for nothing.

The Haitian Maria took him under their wing years ago when he was just a paperboy. Once he met the Trinidadian Mafia he started to see more money and opportunity in dealing with them so he crossed sides knowing the long history of the two families' beef.

Hochoy was sitting on his bedroom floor surrounded by candles, dolls, dice of human organs, and magic cards. This was his daily religion, practiced elements of voodoo. He was talking to dead souls in a special language that sounded like South Africa, IsiZulu language. He was so focused on his worship he didn't see the two men behind him that sneaked in through his terrace balcony he kept open.

Boss kicked Hochoy in the head, knocking him over.

"Ahhh," the black, ugliest nigga Boss had ever seen grunted in pain, staring at the two men dressed in all black with face paint and big assault rifles.

"Your disloyalty led to your death," Lil BD said.

"Let me guess Louis sent you? He's a fucking snake!" Hochoy yelled in bad English because he only knew how to speak Creole and Caribbean Hindustani.

"Bro, look at all this shit. I got a plan," Lil BD said looking at all the TNT bombs and rifles Hochoy had in his room. Hochoy had a habit of collecting bombs and coins since he was a kid.

Boss looked at Lil BD placing live bombs around the room in a line. All the bombs had a timer on them for sixty seconds to activate.

"Nooo!" Hochoy screamed seeing Lil BD turn on all six of the digital bombs.

"You tripping, we got forty-five seconds left," Boss said.

Lil BD shot Hochoy seventeen times. They both heard guards running upstairs yelling in Creole and France. Boss and Lil BD ran to the terrace and climbed down the rope. Shots could be heard when they landed on the ground running at full speed.

Less than ten seconds later, the mansion blew up knocking both men on the ground from the powerful impact.

"Damn, you good?" Boss asked Lil BD who was dizzy.

"Yeah, come on. We out," Lil BD said looking at the eruption of high flames like wildfires.

Once back on the boat they were sailing back down the Pitch Lake.

"Whose idea was that?" Luc asked.

"Mine," Lil BD claimed.

"Good, I see you used your surroundings as a perfect scapegoat. It won't always be that easy," Luc said walking while Lil BD mocked his accent.

Chapter 12

Downtown, Chi-Town

Jenny got off the elevator on her floor ready to get some sleep for the long day she had ahead of her tomorrow. She had plans to help her cousin move to Ohio early in the morning, so she wanted to be well-rested. As she walked inside her condo she heard music playing from her bedroom be Boys II Men. She ran into her kitchen and grabbed the biggest knife out of her counter drawer. She walked slowly to see her door, it was wide open and the strong scent of her cherry Yankee candles could be smelled throughout the house.

When she saw Lil BD standing in the middle of her floor in a suit, clean-cut, and holding a dozen white roses she broke down and started crying like a baby.

"Come here, baby. I love you!" he said now hugging her and holding her.

"I missed you so much," she said as he wiped her tears.

"I'm here now," he said, lifting her chin, seeing her true beauty that he'd fallen in love with before kissing her lips.

"Are you staying or leaving again?"

"I gotta go to Miami to handle some shit. A lot of things been going on. My mom has been kidnapped by a Cartel family. Now we have to go out to Miami and find a way to get her back," he said, turning down her stereo system.

"We?"

"Me and your brother," he replied and things got silent.

"How did that happen?"

"We was both snatched by the Haitian Mafia."

"Oh, my God! For real?"

"Yeah, but it's crazy because they're my family that I never met. My grandfather and uncles, now me and Boss are a part of the Haitian Mafia."

"Wow! Does he know I tried to kill him?" she asked sadly, regretting trying to kill her own brother even though he did kill her father.

"He knew it was you before I even told him."

"What did he say?

"He can't wait to meet you, but I'ma fly you out to Miami once I get settled. It's wartime so I need you to be ready and on point when you're down there."

"I will, I promise. For now, let's enjoy the night," she said standing up in front of him taking off her blouse and jeans.

Lil BD stripped-down looking at her perfect shape. "Nah, keep the heels on, baby," he said sitting on the edge of her bed with his legs wide open.

Jenny got on her knees, stroking his massive dick while licking the tip before she slowly glided her mouth up and down his shaft at a snail pace.

"Ummm," he moaned watching her go deeper and deeper. He spread his legs wide as the tip of his dick thrust to the back of her throat.

She moved her head faster and faster while slurping and sucking. Lil BD wanted to shed a tear. Her head game was so vicious.

"Shit, I'm about to cum," He moaned.

Jenny sucked his tip making popping sounds while massaging his balls until he exploded in her mouth. She slurped all his cum out of the tip and played with it leaving a trace all over her face, hands, and hair.

Lil BD still sat at the edge of the bed while she turned around and slowly eased on his hard dick. She had to loosen her tight slippery walls to adjust to the length and width of his penis.

"Ohhh, yesss, fuck this big dick," he moaned watching Jenny bounce her ass up and down, her ass was clapping on his pelvis area as if she was dancing on the dick to a beat.

"I'm cumming, daddy!" she yelled, bouncing harder on his dick almost breaking it. When she came his dick was covered in creamy goodness. When he pulled out, she swallowed him. He gripped her head and fucked her cute face going deeper into her mouth until tears filled her eyes. He continued to pound into her throat while she wrapped her lips around the shaft causing him to release a load in her mouth, then making her swallow every drop.

Lil BD bent her over and sucked her pussy from behind until he entered her wetness which was dripping out her pussy slit. He gripped her ass cheeks and spread her nice round ass apart going deeper.

"Aaahhh fuckkk, daddy," she screamed arching her back.

Lil BD fucked viciously while talking shit. "Say please," he said long stroking, then short stroking her while grabbing her shoulders forcing her into his dick.

"Pleassseee, I'm cumming!" she screamed biting the pillow catching an orgasm, and squirting all over her bed

"Damn," Lil BD said, seeing her cum squirt out like a pair of waterholes.

They fucked all night until it was time for Lil BD to leave.

***

Southside, Chi-Town

Animal pulled up to Jenny's mom's house in the mailman truck.

"Shut up, nigga!" Animal yelled to the mailman tied up in the back with tape wrapped around his mouth.

Animal saw him making his rounds today and knew it was the perfect time to make his move. Since he'd found out Jenny and Lil BD were a couple she'd been on his shit list and today he was going to send a message.

Animal grabbed a clipboard and a package, then made his way to the front door in a mailman uniform that he'd taken off the original mailman.

He rang the doorbell, then through the window he saw a female approaching when the door opened, he saw a beautiful woman in white, shorts and a tank top showing her flat stomach. Her nana was so phat he couldn't help but stare.

"Up here," Jenny's mom said, smiling, already knowing what he was looking at. She used her sex appeal to catch young niggas all day.

"I have a delivery for you."

"Don't you live down the block?" she said, noticing that the uniform was too tight for him.

Animal pulled his gun from his lower back and shot her four times in the face before walking off down the block into an alley where he'd been parked overnight.

Chapter 13

South Miami, FL

Mayo was in a hole in the wall strip club alone while his guards waited for him in a Porsche limo parked out front. He watched women climb up on poles, twerk on stage, and dance all over the place on clients. This was his first time in this club. It was mostly Cuban women but they weren't allowed to get naked in the club for someone unlike other clubs where bitches were butt naked.

Mayo was in his mid-thirties, tall and skinny with long hair. He was from Peru but had been living in Miami for some time now. He was down with the Peru Cartel Family, he was the underboss working for his uncle Victor.

Since he'd arrived in the club, he'd been watching a tall, Spanish chick with a big ass and tits dance on stage. She looked like a Barbie doll with a lot of makeup but her body was crazy. He sat in the VIP section drinking Patron when he saw her coming his way.

"Hey, papi, can I join?" she said in a soft voice. She was wearing a school uniform, she sat her ass on his small dick and it hardened. "Ummm," she said. "You like what you see, papi?"

"Yeah," he replied as she danced to Spanish music blaring through the speakers.

"At one-thousand dollars and you can have me all night. I can even give you a taste test," she said playing in her hair while grinding on his dick.

Mayo squeezed her big DD breasts feeling his hormones rush to the head of his dick. "Give me a taste," he said looking at her large lips that she'd had botox done on twice.

She got up and pulled his dick out that was the same size as her pinky. She looked at him and his dick, raising her eyebrows.

I've had worse, she thought to herself before sucking the dick with her phat lips. She sucked his dick at a fast speed, deep throating his dick and balls.

"Ummm fuck! Suck that shit," he moaned.

She was going crazy on his dick.

"I'm about to nut, baby," he moaned before he climaxed in less than a minute and his dick went limp. She was disappointed as she swallowed his seeds.

"Let's get out of here," Mayo said searching for his clothes.

Five minutes later they were in his limo with his guards in the front behind the door shutter.

"Get naked," he said.

"Can we do oral and anal? I'm on my period," she said taking off her blouse and bra showing her large bouncy, round breasts.

"Okay," he said undressing.

She turned around and got on all fours lifting her skirt and pushing her thongs to the side. Mayo saw her tiny asshole and licked it making her moan in pleasure before he entered her backdoor. He slid in her ass hole with ease, it was deep and open as if his whole arm could fit in there.

"Yes, fuck me, papi, hard!" she yelled faking as the limo rode through Miami streets. He continued to fuck her roughly. "Stop—hold on," she cried while he continued to pound her back out until he saw brown shit covering his head

"What the fuck?" he said realizing she'd shitted on him.

Mayo then tried to slide in her pussy, he didn't care if she was on her period. When he went under her ass hole, he felt something out of the ordinary making her jump forward.

"I think that's enough for now," she said, pulling her skirt down nervously. "How about I give you some more head?" she said seeing the crazy look on his face.

Mayo pulled out his gun and pointed it at her, seeing the fear of God in her eyes. He reached under her skirt feeling a dick and balls tucked in a jockstrap.

"I'm sorry, I was going to ask you to let me suck your dick to make it right. Put the gun down, I know you like it, papi," she said pleading.

Boc! Boc! Boc! Boc! Boc! Boc! Boc!

Mayo shot her in her forehead so many times that her head bounced with each bullet. His guards rolled down the back window to see what was going on

"Drop this bitch off," Mayo said, pissed that he'd just got tricked by a transgender. In Miami, there were a lot of trannies some looked like models and could fool anybody.

Mayo felt nasty and disgusted. He used her skirt to wipe her shit off his dick.

***

Dode Canty, FL

The next morning Mayo arrived early for his meeting with Chloe in a hotel restaurant. Since Victor was in Peru, Mayo normally handled all the family business affairs.

Chloe walked in with six goons behind her. "Mayo, hi, it's been forever," Chloe said hugging him.

"You look bad," Mayo said, seeing the bags under her eyes.

Normally she was always on her diva shit. He'd always wanted to fuck her, but he knew fucking her came with a price.

"I've been having a lot going on. I'm sure you heard from your boss?" she said, taking a deep breath.

"I heard you killed Manuel's crew muthafuckers. Is that true?"

"No, I claim all my attacks everybody knows that but he sent some of his people at me, so I have no choice but to apply pressure back," she said. Noticing the strange look on his face.

"What?"

"Nothing, I'm just impressed with your strategy tactics. I remember how you went against the Cubans, Brazilians, and the Africans and you're still here breathing, and still sexy," he said.

"Thank you, Mayo. You know how to get my little pussy wet but you're too scared to come get it. The door has always been open for you. I'm sure you heard how good it is," she said in a low pitched voice.

"I have but I was never into suicide. Now how can I be your help, because I'm a little busy Chloe ?"

"Just wanted to speak to you about restart shipments. I need you, it's a drought and I've been good business since we came together."

"I know, this is why me and Victor came up with an idea to help you. Because he don't want to leave you for dead, that's not what we're about."

"Thank you so much."

"Hold on, it's not that easy Chloe. We're going to continue to supply you and help aid you in a time of war, but I have to raise the price," he said

"To what? I don't understand," Chloe said with a confused look.

"We will be charging you double."

"Double!"

"Take it or leave it. Dealing with you comes at a bigger price."

"Whatever, just tell me when my shit is ready," she said, standing to leave.

"Can I still get some pussy?" he asked looking at her thick curves.

"I wouldn't fuck your little dick with another bitch's pussy, you, asshole," she said storming out of the hotel restaurant pissed off with her goons on her heels.

Chapter 14

Miami International Airport

Boss and Lil BD landed in Miami ready for their real mission. Luc would be arriving in a week or so, he went to DR to spend time with his wife and kids because he knew what was about to go down could cost him his life.

"If I wasn't married, I know I could fuck all these Spanish bitches," Lil BD said walking through the airport looking at the beautiful women all over the place.

"I know what you mean," Boss said looking at a thick Spanish woman walking in front of him with the biggest ass he'd ever seen.

Ever since Rosie was killed Boss hadn't been able to look or even feel any type of emotion for another woman. He knew nobody could fill her hole, but he also knew he had to move forward and eventually get his dick out of the dirt.

"Let's go get these cars then check into the condo," Lil BD said climbing in the Uber parked in front of the airport behind a limousine.

Boss saw an older Spanish man with four big guards climb into the limo. He could tell the man was somebody with power from the way he walked and his attire. Both men locked eyes before getting inside their vehicles and going opposite directions.

"You think Malik's coming down here?" Lil BD asked looking at the beautiful view of the city.

"I hope so, he could be useful. The more the merrier because we really don't have a clue what we're truly up against."

"Yeah, that's a fact, bro. I just hope them poles is at the spot because I don't like being naked especially in an area I've never been," Lil BD said, shaking his head.

Flying first-class wasn't his idea, Luc thought it would be better instead of taking a private jet. Luc had many ties to Miami his family was the plug to the Miami Zoe Pound and every Haitian Kingpin in the city.

Luc was going to make sure his nephews had access to guns, an army, and any type of aid they needed.

"We're going to be good but until Luc comes down, let's just lay low, hit some clubs, shopping, and beaches. You know regular tourist shit," Boss said as the Uber pulled into a luxury car dealership making him miss his old car dealership.

After less than twenty minutes of looking around the car lot, Lil BD found a red Ferrari 488 Spider with a black and red two-tone interior. Boss saw a new black Aston Martin DBS that he was feeling.

They used credit cards to pay for the cars with new I.D.s and identities that Luc's people had made for them.

"She's nice, bro?" Lil BD said laughing looking at a bad Spanish bitch with long blonde hair and a body with thick curves busting out her jeans.

"Damn, now that's a bad bitch," Boss said watching a woman walk through the lot.

When the woman turned to walk away to her lime green Wraith, her ass looked like two basketballs bouncing.

"You ready to go freak ass nigga?" Boss told his little brother watching the chick come their way, giving them a respectful smile.

She did a double-take on Boss and stopped in the middle of the lot.

Lil BD thought it was a hit the way she just stopped and stared at Boss.

"Tyrell, is that you?" she said, taking off her Chanel sunglasses.

Boss looked at her crazy because nobody outside of his family knew his real name.

The Spanish woman noticed that he was trying to figure out who she was.

"It's me, Lexus. You remember we met last year in the mall? We kicked it at your hotel with your two friends and my girls," she said now face to face with him.

"Wow, you look amazing. How you been? I had no clue that was you," Boss said while she hugged him. Boss smelled the strong scent of her Chanel perfume.

Lil BD looked at Boss and Lexus confused. He had to give it to Boss because Lexus was the type of bitch that would make a nigga stalk her.

"I got my body done a while back by Doctor Miami," she said, spinning around showing her phat ass and nice, big, perky breasts.

Boss remembered her having no ass. "I see. How's life?"

"Great, I focused on college and living my best life. How about yourself?" she asked.

"I'm okay, I'll be out here for a while."

"Oh, good because when you promised to call me and keep in touch, you didn't," she said rolling her eyes.

"I'm sorry I had a lot going on. My wife passed and I was going through a lot."

"Oh, wow I'm sorry to hear that. I'm here if you need someone to talk to."

"Thanks! Oh, this is my brother BD," Boss said while BD just stood there on his phone but he was really sizing up how phat her pussy was.

"Hey," she said waving at him.

"What's your number? I'll give you a call sometime. I'm free for the weekend," Boss said, handing her his smartphone so she could punch her number in.

"How about you just give me a call when you're ready for me handsome," she said, putting her number into his phone, then kissing his cheek and walking off with her sexy strut.

"I know you hit that, she looks like an eater," Lil BD accused.

"Nah, bro, she a good girl with a little money."

"*A little money?* That bitch got a Wraith and a Birkin bag. Nigga she's a dancer," Lil BD said.

"Whatever nigga, I'm not about to explain shit to you, let's go," Boss said climbing in his car pulling off so Lil BD could follow him.

***

Lexus was in the car dealership looking at the window, watching Boss speed into the Miami traffic. She couldn't believe it was him, her body felt weak.

When Boss came to Miami last year, he left a big imprint on Lexus' mind and heart. She'd never met a person like Boss. Everything about him was her ideal man.

Now that he was single, she knew it was her time to get what she deserved, a good man. Because niggas in Miami weren't even worth a second of her time, everybody was self-centered and living a fast life.

Lexus felt sad he'd lost his wife but one woman's loss was a real woman's gain regardless of the situation in her books.

She'd gone on a couple of dates here and there but nothing serious. Maybe a couple of one-night-stands when she needed some quick dick, but it would never go further than that.

Hearing him say he was in Miami awhile brought joy to her. She wanted to ask him where he was staying but she didn't care. Lexus knew how Miami bitches were with outta town niggas with money. So, she had to find a way to get Boss's full attention before one of the thirsty thots did.

Seeing him made her forget why she'd come to the car dealership. Since she'd gotten her body done niggas had been extra thirsty to slide in her DMs and approach her in public. Some niggas would even holler at her with their friend around. Lexus traded in her lime green Wraith for a custom-made pink and black Bugatti Divo that was worth nine-million dollars.

Chapter 15

Cicero, Chi-Town

Kylie and Malik returned from their fourth date out at a music festival concert downtown and drinks. Kylie invited him back to her place in a nice middle-class neighborhood outside of the city in the suburbs.

"I'm going to have a hangover in the morning," Kylie said laughing and stumbling into her house with Malik helping her into the polish living room.

"You almost got us into a fight at the bar, you are crazy," Malik said, taking off her heel, admiring her manicured red toes and sexy legs.

"I thought she said something to you, sorry."

"She said excuse me," Malik said thinking about how Kylie tried to beat the girl up, then her boyfriend a big, black, gorilla nigga popped up. Luckily, Malik defused the situation before it got out of hand.

"You're such a gentleman, Malik. I love everything about you" she said looking into his eyes.

"I feel the same about you."

"I want you so bad," she said kissing his lips.

"Are you sure?"

"Yeah, just don't play with me," she said like a crazy black girl.

"I won't," he said, as she led him into her bedroom.

Malik was deep in her wet pussy, with her thong to the side ripping her walls in seconds.

"Ummmmm shhhiiittt!" she screamed, digging her nails into his chiseled back. Her legs were pushed all the way back while he stroked in and out of her pussy.

"You like that dick?" he asked, hitting the bottom as her walls slightly squeezed his dick.

"Ugghhh you hitting my spot!" she screamed biting her lips.

Malik went faster as she pulled him closer into her insides.

"Oooohhh, babe, yesss I'm about to—" she moaned, climaxing.

Malik pulled out after she came, she engulfed his dick, bopping her head deep on his pole.

Her head game was so amazing he had to stop before he nutted. He rolled her over, then bent her over, spreading her thighs, staring at her fat, pink pussy, and tiny asshole. Malik pushed his dick into her, loving the way her pussy wrapped around his dick.

"Give it to me hard, Daddy! Fuck that pussy," she cried, grinding her hips back and reaching a quiet orgasm.

Malik was blowing her mind the way he was fucking her. She'd never been fucked so good in her life. He nutted on her nice ass then went down on her, opening her vagina with his tongue. Malik forced his tongue in and out of her pussy with care.

"Oh, my God! Yessss, do that shit, daddy!"

"I'm cumming!" she yelled trying to catch her breath as her legs started to shake.

Kylie was sexually drained but she was in the mood to suck some more dick. She laid him down and gulped his dick up and down spitting on his cock, showing out. She worked his dick for forty minutes straight like she didn't have a jawbone.

Once he came inside her throat, she rode his dick to the reverse cowgirl position. The night was full of passionate sex.

***

Miami, FL

Malik arrived in Miami early, he did a little sight-seeing on South Beach. This was his second time, last time him, Boss, and Animal had a blast hitting up clubs, beaches, and shopping.

"This gotta be it," Malik said to himself looking at the expensive condos in front of him.

It was hard to leave Kylie because homegirl's pussy and head game was on the next level, but he knew he had to come to Miami to hold Boss down, he was his other half. Malik got off on the 10th floor to see Boss's crib to his left. He knocked twice hearing the Lil

Bibby music, playing inside the crib. Malik knocked two more times and heard the music turned down a little.

Boss knew he was in town because he called him when he landed hours ago.

When the door opened, he saw Lil BD standing there smoking a blunt and staring at him, before opening the door and walking off.

"Malik, what's up?" Boss yelled from the kitchen, happy to see his best friend. Both men hugged tightly as if they hadn't seen each other in years.

"You look older, Joe," Malik said sitting on a stool in the kitchen watching Boss warm up some leftover pizza.

"It's just the beard but we got a room for you down the hall it's four rooms in this bitch. Walk-in closets in every room, private bathrooms, a big balcony, a game room upstairs, and downstairs. Make yourself at home. Glad to have you but I gotta update you everything that's going on."

"A'ight but what's up with BD? I ain't gotta worry about him trying to take my head off, do I?" Malik said laughing but was as serious as a heart attack.

"Ask him," Boss said, looking behind him at Lil BD standing there.

"I should be asking you the same thing, Lord," Lil BD said standing behind him with a bottle of Henny in his hand.

"We good, the past is the past. I ain't tripping but the only reason you're still breathing is because of Boss."

"I should be thankful then, huh?" Lil BD said walking off with a smirk.

"Y'all two niggas are just alike," Malik said.

"That's the bro. What you been up to?"

"Laying low with wifey," Malik said, surprising Boss as he turned around giving his full attention.

"*Wifey?* Who got you open, bro? I thought I would never see this day. Shit you giving me hope."

"Someone you know very well."

"Come on with the mystery shit, bro, spill the shit."

"Kylie," Malik said making Boss spill his Pepsi all over the floor

"White girl, red hair, my ex-employee, sexy walk?"

"Yep."

"She tell you where I found her? She is a good girl, bro."

"I know everything, but I can't judge her off her past, feel me?"

"Facts as long as you're happy, bro. Just wear a condom," Boss said joked.

"You ain't got nobody special since—you know Rosie?"

"I do."

"Okay, you remember the slim, cute, Spanish chick?"

"Hell yeah, she was bad. What's good with her?"

"She's looking like eye candy. Shorty got her body done somethin' crazy. I ain't even recognize her when I saw her hop out of the Wraith at a car dealership."

"Damn, that's a good look. I can tell she got a bag," Malik said.

"Y'all trying to go out to club G5 tonight? A chick told me about it yesterday. It's two stripper bitches that live downstairs," Lil DB said, pulling up a stool next to Malik.

"I'm down," Malik said, and Boss shook his head.

***

Mexico City, Mexico

Nueva was in his large walk-in closet dragging money out of one of his safes while his goons waited for him downstairs. He was on his way to a meeting in the Philippines with very powerful government officials who wanted to purchase some heroin.

For over thirty years he'd run the Mexican Cartel Family out of Mexico City, the state capital and most dangerous area in Mexico.

Nueva was an old man with a thick mustache and glasses. At the age of sixty-three, he was living on his last leg with lung cancer, but he still managed to travel and run his organization.

The recent loss of his son crushed him deeply but what really did it, was when he received the roses and note from Chloe basically claiming his son murder.

Once he had his travel money, he was ready to leave. He never left his home without 250,000 in cash on him.

Nueva made his way to his backyard with six guards leading him to his helipad in the middle of his land stretching out for miles on a wide grass field. He climbed on his private helicopter ready for takeoff. When they were in the sky Nueva was talking to his goons in Spanish making jokes.

Ten minutes into the air Nueva asked his personal bodyguard something in Spanish, but he didn't reply. The pilot then did the unthinkable and took the car keys out of the transmissions making the helicopter slowdown in mid-air. Nueva started yelling in Spanish but the pilot opened his door and took off his helmet.

When Nueva saw his face, he pulled out his gun because it wasn't the pilot but RJ from the Columbia Cartel. RJ jumped out before he had a chance to fire a shot. RJ sneaked onto his land earlier, killed his pilot, and stole his outfit. He loved skydiving so this was a party for RJ. When he got closer to the ground he pulled out his parachute. Nueva's helicopter crashed 100 yards away from him in the mountains, killing all seven men.

Chapter 16

Sarasota, FL

The crew was at a real shooting range with assault rifles they never heard of lined up in private booths, aiming at their target sheets.

"Fire," Luc said, walking behind Boss, Lil BD, and Malik watching their target practice. The men all emptied a fifty round clip mag, then reloaded and waited on another sheet to appear down the aisle.

"Stop, that's enough let's see who won," Luc said, taking off his ear muffles and looking at the digital scoreboard on the TV screen, seeing that Lil BD had come in first and Boss and Malik were tied. All of them had above-average scores so Luc was cool with that.

"Good job now it's time for a swimming lesson," Luc said.

"You know niggas can't swim," Lil BD said.

"Today you will because it may save your life one day. Trust me, I know," Luc said thinking back to when he was kidnapped by the Tobago Mafia and woke up on a boat. Luc was able to fight his way off the boat and dive into the Caribbean Sea. He swam for almost two days to make it back to Haiti.

***

Downtown, Chi-Town

Jerry left her doctor's office where she found out that she was pregnant which surprised her because she'd only had sex one time, in months and that was with Lil BD when he came to see her. She was scared to tell her husband. What if he denied her being pregnant by him because he'd only fucked once? The night he came back he nutted in her so many times she lost count. It only took one time to make a baby and she wasn't a part of the abortion crew. Jenny was totally against killing unborn seeds; she even attended six protests at college on that topic.

Jenny planned to just call Lil BD when she got to tell him the news. If he was to trip or act up, unlike most black women she wasn't going to take him to court or put him on child support because she could take care of her own. That's what being a strong black woman all about.

***

University of Miami College

Candice sat in the school lunchroom going over some homework for her next class while on her lunch break eating a Vegan sandwich. Candice was short, classy, and petite, with green eyes, thick eyebrows, bronze skin, and long black and brown hair that she wore in a bun. She was a full-blooded Peruvian, born in Peru's capital Lima and raised in Miami Beach. Her father was Victor the Pero Cartel boss she was his youngest daughter.

Studying to become a scientist Candice was a genius, one of the smartest women in the school. At twenty-two years old she was mature and building her own way in life unlike her older sister Julienne who was in the family business at the age of twenty-four.

Candice felt like her college was below her standards, but it was the closest college to her father, and he wanted her to stay close.

The only friend she had in the school was Lexus the two chilled all day at school and sometimes off-campus. Candice wasn't really a party girl, but Lexus was. A couple of months ago they'd gone out for Lexus's birthday and Candice got alcohol poisoning at a bar on South Beach.

She was single because her type was hard to come by especially the way her pops put her on a chain. She liked blacks, mostly thugs with good hearts. She had a thing for jail niggas, to her there was nothing sexier than a big, muscled chocolate nigga coming home from a bid.

Realizing her class started in five minutes she gathered all her items and left. Spanish dudes tried to holler at her on her way out but she paid them no mind and walked faster with her head down hugging her textbooks on her way to the Science, Tech build.

***

Buenaventura, Columbia

RJ's wife Del Rey was a tall Colombian woman with a pale white complexion but she was a Latina woman who only spoke Spanish. She ran five to ten miles every morning on a trail in the woods behind her house.

She made it back home tired and out of breath, she just wanted to eat breakfast, shower, and clean the house. This was her everyday daily routine. She was a housewife just like her mother, grandmother, and eight sisters.

Marrying RJ made her give up her dreams of becoming a model and Colombia actress. Every day she regretted marrying him because he treated her badly and he cheated on her daily. RJ even had the nerve to bring women into their bed four times, claiming they should spice up their sex life but one of the women was her blood sister.

As she walked into the front door she took her earbuds out of her ears and made her way to the state-of-the-art kitchen designed for chefs to prepare meals. The mansion was 18,817 square feet, with marbled flooring, 18th Century French onyx, French doors, spiral ceilings, eight rooms, and six private walk-in bathrooms.

Del Rey walked into her kitchen and was attacked by four, large, Spanish men in suits. She tried to run but one of the goons grabbed her hair slamming her down onto the floor, hard.

"Ahhh," she grunted looking up at the four men standing over her with guns.

A man walked up to her and asked her in Spanish where was RJ? When she replied that she hadn't seen him in days he knew she was worthless. He knew she was telling the truth because he had his goons watching her for five days now.

"Okay, then thank you," Mark said before firing ten shots in her frail chest, then leaving.

Mark was from the Santos Cartel, he was the family capo and very dangerous. He was thirty-two, evil, cocky, smart, and a mastermind in the time of war.

He was from the slums of Givaudan one of the worst parts in Colombia where he learned how to kill and survive. Hector saved him and blessed him with a better life and way of living. Mark loved Hector like a father he never had because he taught him everything he knew in life. The only real family he had was a younger brother who he hadn't seen in seventeen years. He had a girlfriend, but he kept his private life away from his business it was the first thing Hector taught him in the game besides loyalty.

Chapter 17

Miami, FL

Boss entered the Bar & Grill restaurant dressed to impress looking around for Lexus. The place was full tonight, waiters were shoulder to shoulder serving guests and taking orders. He saw Lexus in the far back sitting by herself in a red dress, looking stunning from afar. He and Lexus talked on the phone for days. When she asked him to come on a friendly date, he couldn't deny it. There was something about her that he really liked, her energy was very strong and to make it worst she was a dime piece.

"You look so nice," Lexus said standing to hug him, checking out his attire and nice diamonds.

"Thanks but you look like you're ready to take a bitch's man in this joint," he said sitting down pecking at her perfect round breast sitting firmly in her dress just giving off enough view to make a nigga thirsty.

"What you been up? I ordered our food," she said.

"How do you know I like what you like?"

"Because I ordered us what you like shrimp, lobster tails, oysters, fried rice, and baked chicken breast," she said looking at his gesture, knowing she'd hit it on the point.

"My favorite foods. Who you work for?" Boss said, making her laugh.

"I just listen well. When you came down here last time. I absorbed everything you said, that's how you get to know people."

"At least someone listens, but you don't have no special somebody in your life. I'm not trying to get gunned down in these streets over a beautiful woman that's not even mine," he said right after their food arrived.

"I'm single, Ty. If I wasn't, I wouldn't even have entertained you. I'm not that type of girl, I'm loyal. A lot of people misjudge a beautiful woman for being like the rest of these shady bitches out here."

"I just don't want to waste my time or yours because I live a—" he was cut off by her hand pausing him.

"I don't care what type of life you live as long as I can be a part of it, and you don't hurt me. Since the night I met you, Ty, I could never get you out of my head. The crazy shit is I've never shared a connection with another soul the way I do with you," she said.

Boss read her eyes and saw them get a little glossy. He saw the truth in her eyes, he couldn't lie to himself, he'd thought about her since the first time they met, even when he was with Rosie.

"My wife was recently killed and I'm still healing an open wound. I don't think that would be fair to you."

"I know what's fair to me and being without you isn't. I will help you heal. That's what I'm here for, Ty. You don't have to suffer alone no more," she said.

I believed every word she said and leaned in towards her kissing her soft red lips.

"So, I guess I'm wifey?" she said, licking her lips.

"I wouldn't have it no other way."

***

Santiago, Dominican Republic

Luc was in the limo with his wife getting his dick sucked on his way to his wife's father's crib.

"Mmmmm," she moaned, taking his dick down her throat the way she knew he liked. She came back up doing tongue tricks on the head of his dick.

Lela slurped his pre-cum while engulfing him again using her thick lips to message his pole. The way she sucked dick felt like she had no teeth. After twenty minutes, he shot a load in her throat. The limo pulled up to the large gate in front of Lela's father's house surrounded by armed men patrolling the early 19th Century castle made from stones.

"You got a stain right there just a little drip," Luc said pointing to his wife's chin where semen was hanging and about to fall on her dress.

"Oh, no," she said grabbing a napkin and wiping her mouth and chin. The limo came to a stop in her father's long driveway. "You're so crazy, papi, and nasty. Just how I like it," she said in her Spanish accent before getting out.

Lela's father Danilo had arranged a sit-down today for the time because the two men weren't too fond of each other. Dominican men looked down on their daughters marrying Haitian men or Puerto Rican's due to the history of their culture.

Per Cantra Danilo had respect for Luc because of the caliber of person he demonstrated, and he protected his daughter with his own life.

Lela went to help her mother with dinner while Luc led himself upstairs to the third level where Danilo's office was. There were seven rooms on each floor, and they all had French double doors with a guard posted up outside of each one.

Luc knocked on Danilo's doors and he could smell the aroma of cigar smoke.

Pueblo opened the doors giving Luc a quick nod before walking off and all the guards in the hallway followed in a rush. Pueblo was the family businessman, enforcer, and killer. He wasn't even twenty years old yet, but his name was heavy in certain places.

"Luc have a seat," Danilo said in English standing by his file cabinet, looking out the window at his beautiful garden out back that he took pride in.

Danilo was the face and boss of the Dominican Cartel who controlled a lot of the drugs entering the East Coast, especially the New York and New Jersey areas.

His older brother Cadeno started the family business when they were coming up in the treacherous section of San Pedro de Macoris, a small city near Santo Domingo.

After Cadeno gave his little brother a position and a seat at his table, his body was found floating in the Lago Enriquillo ocean. When Danilo killed his own brother to climb to the top of the heir everybody had no choice but to bow down. Danilo built his army from the ground up and made alliances with the Cuban Cartel family who supplied him with drugs.

That was over thirty years ago, now Danilo was the one supplying the Cuban Cartel after Perez died and his son took over.

"What's going on, Danilo? How you been?" Luc said crossing his legs and resting his hand on his knee.

"All is well, enjoying my life and protecting my investments," Danilo said, turning around, walking to his chair.

Luc knew Danilo well enough to know that every word he said had a meaning to it because he was a man of very few words.

"I'm not understanding."

"Your brother, Louis, is stepping on my toes trying to deal with my people. I mean more than one. Your brother doesn't have the same values as you, Luc."

"So, what do you want me to do? I don't get into my brother's business dealings Danilo, but I will speak to him for you," Luc stated.

"That's all I ask. The only reason why I come to you is because you're my daughter's husband. If it wasn't for that I'm sure you could paint the rest of the picture," Danilo said strongly.

"Sometimes the painting doesn't always come out the way we expect it to, things can be a little messy," Luc added.

"True but, how's Miami?"

"Great, I love catching tans. It's good for my skin."

"I'm sure it is thanks for coming out. I know you're a busy man these days."

"No problem; you're family, Danilo, and a man of respect."

"Thanks, dinner should be ready soon. Let's join the family. First how about I leave you with a word of advice? In the jungle, only two animals survive and the lion is one of them."

"Thanks for the tip, but there is only enough room for one animal in this jungle," Luc said, leaving.

Chapter 18

Buff City, Chi-Town

Malik was back in Chicago for a couple of days to handle something. Malik explained to Kylie the type of life he was into and she begged him to be a part of it. She even quit her job to devote time to becoming a killer. Malik had to explain this wasn't a motion picture movie, Tomb Raider type lifestyle. It was real and either one of them could lose their lives at any second.

"Why you so quiet, babe?" Kylie asked Malik who was looking up the block toward a trap house where some young gangbangers sold coke and molly.

"Shhh! I'm watching something," he replied.

"I'm watching the same shit, babe," Kylie said dressed in all black with a hoodie. "How about I give you some head so you can chill out?"

Malik gave her an evil look letting her know he was serious about his business.

"Just joking, daddy, damn," Kylie said watching the dark block from the Honda Civic.

"You ready? You're up," he said talking to himself because Kylie was already halfway up the block. Roxy was on her way back up the block.

***

Kylie was on the sidewalk walking toward Roxy who was walking at a fast speed.

"Where can I get some coke from?" Kylie asked Roxy, making her hit her breaks and spin around.

Roxy looked her up and down to see if she was an undercover cop because they always sent white girls to set niggas up.

"I've seen you around here before a couple of times but your hair was red," Roxy said remembering Kylie from her hooker days.

91

"Yeah, I used to cat but now I catwalk on the Westside. The Johns pay more," Kylie said.

"How much you got?" Roxy asked with big eyes.

"Fifty."

"Oh, come on, gurl. I'll go back inside and holler at Pa. Then we can go back to my place, I live right there," Roxy said pointing up the block.

"Okay," Kylie said, handing Roxy a fifty-dollar bill.

Roxy ran back into the trap house and brought three fat twenties of coke in sandwich bags and pocketed one of them for herself.

Once back outside Roxy and Kylie went to her crib to get high.

Inside Roxy's house was dirty, nasty, and it had a bad odor inside that would make anyone with a stomach vomit.

"Sorry about the mess," Roxy said, stepping over clothes and beer bottles.

Since her daughter was killed her house had been a mess because her daughter always cleaned up for her. Animal regularly came by some time and he would bring her 100 dollars and some food.

Roxy sat at the dinner table full of trash and old food. "Oh, hell nah not today. You came in the wrong house today muthafucka," Roxy said to five large roach racing on the table. She took off her shoe and started killing each one of them.

Kylie stood there watching trying her hardest not to laugh. Kylie had nights when roaches would crawl all over her body.

"Let's get this party started," Roxy said, pulling out the coke. "Sit down, gurl. You got something to sniff with?" Roxy said looking up to see a gun pointed at her forehead.

"Don't move bitch!"

"I'm sorry I only took an extra twenty you can have it. Please!" she cried.

"I already know that you're trifling bitch."

Boc! Boc! Boc!

Kylie shot her in the head feeling the vibration in her hand felt so good she emptied the whole clip. Kylie walked outside without touching anything to leave no fingerprints, she'd been watching a lot of crime scene shows on HLN.

"Here you go," she said, handing the empty gun to Malik.

"You used the whole clip, babe?"

"Yeah, now let's go fuck I'm horny," she said.

Malik looked at her crazy before pulling off.

***

Miami, FL

Luc was inside Boss and Lil BD just staring at them for a minute straight.

"Is this part of the training?" Lil BD asked sitting on the living room couch.

"One of you has to take one for the team," Luc said.

Boss and Lil BD had no clue what he was talking about. The doorbell rang and Luc went to answer it.

"How this nigga bring company to our crib, bro?" Lil BD asked.

Luc came back into the living room with a black female carrying two suitcases.

"You can set up shop over there," Luc told the woman.

"What's this?" Boss asked.

"One of you will be placed in a mask to look like Chloe for the Cuban hit and the other one will prepare to go hit Mayo. You got a minute to decide because I need Mayo hit in two hours. I'll be back," Luc said walking out of the crib.

***

Lil Havana, Miami

Mayo parked his black Benz Class E 300 in the front of a run-down apartment complex in the middle of the hood full of Cubans and two percent Peruvians. He was meeting with one of his soldiers who sold keys of dope for him and yesterday he was short 100,000 so he came to collect. Mayo walked upstairs quickly noticing that the door was wide open.

"Saint!" Mayo yelled walking inside the dimmed apartment.

When he looked into the small living room area, he saw three dead Spanish men from his circle on the floor bleeding out of their heads. He pulled out his gun and did a quick look around the apartment. He found Saint on the toilet in the bathroom dead with a bullet in his head and a sports magazine in his hand.

"Shit," Mayo yelled, touching the fresh blood on the bathroom floor, knowing the murders were recent so the killers could still be near lurking.

He saw an Ak-47 behind the bathroom door, he grabbed it and left the crib with caution looking all around him.

***

Lil BD sat in the boarded-up, abandoned crib across the street watching Mayo's every move. He'd killed four of his men less than ten minutes ago.

Luc gave him Mayo's trap house locations and all four were located in Lil Havana. Lil BD chose to hit this one first unaware that Mayo was coming.

When Lil BD saw Mayo's Benz, he was in his Range about to pull off onto his next mission. Seeing the abandoned building across the street he went in, hid, and watched Mayo's every move outside.

He saw Mayo come out with an Ak-47, he knew it was now or never. It was very dark on the dead-end street, but Lil BD lined his Draco up to Mayo's head.

Tat! Tat! Tat! Tat! Tat! Tat!

Mayo ducked the bullets right on time coming from across the street. He fired his chopped back tearing up the old house.

Lil BD almost got hit before he returned fire. Lil BD rained bullets toward Mayo hitting him in his arm before he hit the ground taking cover, trying to get to his Benz crawling. Lil BD saw that he was trying to get to the Benz and got up and ran outside.

By the time he made it outside all he saw was the Benz's tail lights at the end of the block speeding off. Lil BD got in the Range cursing himself for not having patience and waiting for him to get in his car first.

Romell Tukes

Chapter 19

Disneyland, FL

Nandez's wife, Sherri, was out enjoying the beautiful day at Disneyland with her young son and daughter.

Sherri was a beautiful, Cuban woman in her mid-forties with a fit toned body, she'd been married to Nandez for twenty-two years. There was no questioning her loyalty and love for Nandez even after he had fathered children outside of their marriage, she was still loyal to him.

The way she was raised was like most Cuban women to submit to their husbands and never leave or cheat on them, if so, it was frowned upon.

"Mommy, can we get on the haunted house ride please?" her eight-year-old son asked tugging on her purse.

"Yeah, mom please," her cute daughter added, giving her puppy dog eyes.

Sherri hated when her kids tag-teamed her for shit because she couldn't deny their cute little faces. Her daughter was ten-years-old and already a brilliant mastermind like her father.

Sherri looked at the long line and took a deep breath while looking at the maid and nanny who came with the kids everywhere they went.

"I will take them," the nanny said, holding both of the kid's little hands.

"I'll come too," Sherri said, walking with them to get in line.

After thirty minutes of waiting in line, all four of them hopped on the train with two other Spanish women who were in line. The train ride only had six seats per train. As they rode inside the scary house, they saw a bunch of clowns and scary monsters jumping out of them.

"Mommy, I'm scared!" Sherri's son yelled, putting his head in her lap.

"It's okay, baby. They're not real," Sherri said as lights flashed through the dark tunnel area with a fake Chucky doll standing there with a knife.

They saw a lady with a gun in her hand dressed in a black army combat suit.

"Mommy, she looks real," the little girl said and the nanny thought the same thing.

"They are all fake." Sherri looked at the woman's face who looked familiar.

Bloc! Bloc! Bloc!

"Mommy!" Sherri's daughter yelled when she saw her mom's head split open.

Bloc! Bloc! Bloc! Bloc! Bloc! Bloc!

The shooter killed both kids leaving the nanny and two Spanish women in fear.

The shooter ran out the back exit leaving the innocent women screaming and mourning over the death of the little kids.

***

The woman dressed in all black made her way through the crowded entrance while police instructed everybody to exit and leave because there'd been a shooting. Inside the parking lot, the woman hopped in a Tahoe truck taking off and pulled the face mask off which was a thick layer.

Boss pulled the extra rubber texture off his face so he could look like his regular self. Luc came up with the idea to have special makeup artists make a mask of Chloe.

***

Westside, Chi-Town

Animal was walking down the street early in the morning with a picture in his hand looking for someone. Since, Animal's mom murder, he'd been on edge and he wanted blood by any means. He'd spoken to Chloe recently and she told him she had a feeling Boss and his little brother was coming for her and setting her up due to their mom being kidnapped.

She told Animal she needed him in Miami. He was flying out there tonight after he handled his affairs. Animal found who he was looking for lying on a cardboard box with a blanket in front of Popeyes Chicken.

"Sir, I need some help in this alley. I got a hundred dollars for you if you can help me move this garbage," Animal told the old man who was in bad shape for smoking crack for twenty years.

"Hell yeah, youngin', I got it," the homeless man said sitting up in a rush.

Animal smelled the strong odor of shit coming from his body.

"Right here," Animal said, pointing at a big green dumpster.

"Shit where you want this?"

"Right there is good," Animal said, pulling out a 40-Glock, shooting Lil BD's dad in his neck five times and leaving him slumped behind the dumpster.

"I did you a favor," Animal said then walked off.

***

Golden Beach, FL

Nandez received the news of his family's gruesome murder and emotions filled his heart. Losing his wife and kids was a sharp pain, he never thought he would have to experience.

"Bring her in here," Nandez told two of his guards standing in the living room of Nandez's marvelous mansion.

Nandez sat on his couch in deep thought wondering how he would cross these lines. At forty-two years old he'd been around the block a couple of times and he kept his enemy close so he could smell them plotting before they strike.

He was Cuban with a bloodline of bosses from his father, to his grandfather, and great grandfather. He was very short, dark-skinned, and fat with a big bankroll.

Nandez quickly thought the killing of his family was from Danilo because he was not buying coke from Louis or the Haitian Mafia.

"Here she is, boss," his guards said, walking the nanny inside the living room with her ankles and hands tied.

Nandez didn't know what had happened at Disneyland except his family was murdered and the maid/nanny was still alive. It didn't make sense to him, but he was going to get to the bottom of it.

"Mr. Nandez, I swear I didn't have nothing to do with this. I been around here for twenty years," she said in very bad English because she'd spent her whole life in Cuba until two years ago when Nandez came to Florida.

"I know you didn't, but who did?" he asked.

"It was a woman. I saw her before she came to visit you in Cuba. I remember her face, beautiful woman."

"Are you sure?"

"Yes, I'm certain I believe she only spared me to relay the killing."

"Did she look Cuban?"

"No, she was Colombian," she said remembering the woman's face.

Nandez got up and whispered something in one of his guard's ear before the big man walked off. "If I was to show you a picture would you be able to tell me if it's the woman or not?"

"Si," she replied.

One of the guards walked back into the room handing Nandez a picture frame. "Does she look familiar?" Nandez said passing the picture frame to her.

"Oh, my God! Si-si-si!" she yelled crying.

Nandez was pissed, he couldn't believe Chloe had murdered his family. They took a picture together years ago, the two families had always been on good terms until now. He had his men untie the nanny and he went to make some calls, he vowed to kill Chloe if it was the last thing he did.

***

South Miami, FL

Hitler arrived in Miami days ago he was staying at a lowkey hotel in Liberty City in the hood. He was riding in an orange McLaren 570s Spider just to blend in because everybody had a Foreign car in the city. The lowest a nigga would go is a Benz or BMW.

He was on a mission to find Boss since finding Malik in Chicago was like looking for a ghost and he wasn't no ghostbuster.

It was nighttime and the streets were full of people on Broadway leaving in and out of clubs and bars, partying.

In Miami, Hitler knew every outta town nigga was going out clubbing especially in the crazy strip clubs and regular clubs. He knew it wouldn't be hard to find Lil BD or Boss because he knew their movements.

He parked behind a GMC truck across from the packed bar he was about to go into. When he climbed out of his car a candy red BMW i8 pulled up to park behind him, but Hitler saw the car was closing in to close.

The front bomber of the BMWi8 slammed into the back of the McLaren putting a dent in it as it backed up.

"What the fuck wrong with you, nigga, you blind?" Hitler yelled ready to beat the shit out of the driver.

Seconds later the driver got out in slow motion. When Hitler saw heels and a nice set of toes and legs hit the pavement, he knew it had to be a bitch.

"I'm so-so-so sorry," a beautiful Spanish woman said with a slur in her voice. "I'll pay for it, the price don't matter. I'm just so sorry."

"You must be drunk? Don't worry about it," he replied looking at how flawless and sexy she looked in her white Dior dress with her back and stomach area cropped out on the dress.

"No, please I can pay for it."

"No, it's okay, you're good," Hitler said, liking her Spanish accent. "What's your name?"

"Candice! How about you?" she said looking him up and down seeing he was a cutie.

"Hitler, I'm from Chicago but I'm down here visiting."

"Tourist, huh in a nice car?"

"Was a nice car," he added, looking at his bumper.

"Sorry about that but I don't normally go out. My friend Lexus was supposed to meet me here but she got so drunk at the last bar, I believe she went home. Since I'm out I wanted to enjoy myself. How about you come get drinks on me?" she said, showing her winning smile.

"Okay, but you look a little too young to be drinking."

"Thanks, but I'm legal. Now come on," she said walking across the street to the bar.

Hitler and Candice spent hours together hanging out and having a great time. Hitler found out she was a smart college girl, and she was Peruvian. He'd never met a chick from Peru but he had to admit they had some exotic bitches after meeting Candice.

Chapter 20

North Miami, FL

Meanwhile, across town, Lexus called Boss over to her condo to chill and drink with her. They'd been spending a lot of time together for the last couple of days and Lexus was loving every second of it. She'd been out drinking all night since the evening with Candice but was too drunk to continue to party. Boss rang her buzzer from downstairs and she let him in. She looked at herself in her hallway mirror checking out her new lingerie and net leggings. Then she rushed to open the door with her heart racing because tonight was the night that she planned to give herself to him.

"You look—damn," Boss said, staring at her breasts and large nipples which were both pierced.

"Follow me," she said, leading him to the master bedroom.

Boss looked around the colorful condo seeing a lot of Japanese artwork, glass ceilings, a balcony, a large carpeted living room with new, white, leather furniture, and an amazing dining room area connected to the kitchen.

In the room, the soft music of Jhene Aiko played in the background setting the mood. She began to undress him starting from the bottom up to see how incredibly hard he was.

"I'm happy to see you, too. You have no clue," she said taking off his shirt, then her lingerie and climbing into her bed.

Boss wasted no time sucking on her big breasts and sliding a finger into her soaking tight slit which was freshly shaved.

"Mmmm," she moaned and squirmed.

"Can I taste you?"

"Please, baby," she said watching him go further down caressing her soft curvy body.

When his thick lips and tongue met her swollen clit, it didn't take her long to cum hard. Boss stuck his throbbing dick into her tight sex box trying to work his way inside of her never feeling pussy so tight in his life.

Lexus' pussy was so tight it was hurting his dick. He tried loosening her up but she felt so good, warm, and tight. Boss had to really control himself because she had knock out pussy.

She moved her hips to his rhythm while moaning in pleasure feeling him getting deep inside her.

"Ugghhh, yesss!" she screamed making him pick up the pace turning him on by her sexy noises.

Minutes later she caught a double orgasm. Lexus wanted to return the favor of oral sex because she was considered a giver. She got in a sixty-nine position and spit on his dick before slowly guiding him down her throat. Boss was sucking on her pussy while feeling her mouth work his dick in a slow-motion making his toes curl.

Boss couldn't hold off any longer. "I'm cumming, baby!" he yelled while she jerked him off until he shot out thick cum all over her face. She licked and kissed his dick until it was time for her to ride his dick.

She rode his dick for twenty minutes before she was drained and needed a break. They had sex five times before they tapped out like a UFC fighter.

***

Bogota, Columbia

"Wake up, bitch," Chloe said, throwing hot water on Janella's face that was swollen from days of beating.

"Ahhh!" Janella yelled feeling the hot water scorch her face waking her up.

"Now tell me why your sons are! They're trying to set me up. How do they even know it's me, that has you?" Chloe asked Janella who was silent.

"I have no clue what you're referring to."

"Oh, I see hardball. Well, if they don't stop soon I'ma kill you and them. I can't see them doing all this shit by themselves. They're not that smart, trust me," Chloe said studying Janella's expression.

Mayo told her the Cuban Cartel ordered a hit on her because she killed his family. She was shocked to hear the news because she'd just recently taken out the Mexican City Cartel and now it was Nandez.

She knew the only person it could be was Boss because of Janella. What she didn't understand was how Boss knew to kill the most dangerous Cartel families. He was a Chicago kid from the ghetto.

There was no way he could know how to kill the most dangerous men in the world without help, she thought.

"I'ma find out what's really going on. And I'ma make you wish you were never born", Chloe said getting up to leave.

"Too late," Janella said lying in soaked sheets.

***

Ibague, Columbia

RJ was in the passenger seat of a Jeep Wrangler with no doors on his way home after visiting his mom. The recent death of his wife took a toll on him, but he'd already moved her sister into their house. Her sister was a big freak and RJ always loved everything about her and her pussy and oral sex was special.

Chloe told him about Nandez's family being killed and he was accusing her. There was so much shit going on RJ was starting to think Chloe was really killing all these people.

RJ knew his sister and he could see her doing everything she was being accused of because she was a snake with a venomous bite. He didn't know what she was going to do with the Cuban Cartel, but he wanted no parts he had good business ties with Nandez's little brother.

Since killing the Mexican Cartel boss he'd been with security because he didn't trust nobody or nothing around him.

He made it to his estate then mayhem filled the driveway.

Tat! Tat! Tat! Tat! Tat! Tat! Tat! Tat! Tat!

A group of snipers hiding all over RJ house popped out killing his guards. RJ grabbed his gun and started shooting back hitting one of the snipers in the chest making him fall on his back.

Another sniper shot RJ twice in his knees making him fall and his gun fly across the pavement. Two men rushed RJ and grabbed him, then dragged him into his open garage.

"Pleaseee, I've done nothing wrong," RJ cried men tears.

The man tied his hands to a thick pipe in the middle of the floor. Seven men opened the door from inside coming out. They were all waiting for RJ to come inside, they'd already killed his wife's sister.

Torres came face to face with RJ shaking his head dressed in a gray tuxedo, brushing his slick hair back. Torres was Nandez's little brother and he was very sick in the head, had been since he was a kid. He was good for business, but the only issue was he didn't talk, he wrote things down on paper for people.

RJ saw him writing something down on a piece of yellow paper. When RJ was handed the paper and read it. He begged for his life. *You Die Now.* The paper read.

Torres saw an electric chainsaw hanging on the wall and grabbed it. Once he turned it on Torres did a bow like they do in China when greeting royalty.

"No, please, Chloe did it, not me!" he screamed before Torres put the sharp chainsaw edges on his neck with pressure.

Torres began sawing off his neck like he was in the woods cutting trees. Blood squirted all over the place while Torres was focused and in his own zone. A couple of the guards closed their eyes. Torres always went beyond kill mode. The shit he did to victims made Jason, Freddy, Chucky, and the BTK killer all look like angels. When he was done Torres left with the chainsaw.

Chapter 21

Miragoane, Haiti

Francisque closed his eyes while his private G6 jet was due to land in five minutes from his trip from Libya. Things had been going good for the boss, other than his missing daughter. He'd just received information on his daughter's location from an old friend who had strong ties before Francisque killed him.

He was very proud of Boss and Lil BD, there was no doubt in his mind they were his grandkids. Today he planned to call a family meeting so he could tell them where Janella was being held so they could form a plan to get his baby back at any cost.

Due to all the drama Chloe was encountering with the Mexicans, the Cubans, and the Santos Cartel he was sure she would have her hands tied, so right now was the perfect time to get his daughter home safe. Being in the game for as long as he'd been he knew Chloe wouldn't kill Janella until she got whatever it was she wanted.

The jet landed hard on the private strip because the thick, gloomy fog made it hard to see.

"Francisque, the truck is out there," one of his security guards stated.

"They're early today," Francisque replied in Creole.

The weather was bad outside this morning but that was because Haiti was expecting a big tropical storm within the next couple of hours. Francisque stepped off the jet to see dark, gray clouds and heavy fog. Three all-black SUVs awaited him in a line as always, he was well protected at times.

Men dressed in all black and ski masks exited the SUVs with assault rifles.

Francisque caught on quickly because the license plates to all the SUVs were off so he knew the trucks didn't belong to his men.

Boom! Boom! Boom! Boom!

Francisque was the first to shoot, taking out two gunmen while he was on one knee, firing.

Tat! Tat! Tat! Tat! Tat! Tat! Tat! Tat!

The goons fired their assault rifles taking out Francisque's security team with ease.

Francisque endured in the gun battle shooting another gunman in the head with his last bullet in his 9mm. He quickly reached for his .38 special in his ankle holster.

"Don't fucking do it," a female voice said standing behind him with a gun to his head. Chloe sneaked up behind him during the gun battle, emerging from out of the woods.

"Chloe, good to see you again," Francisque said, feeling rain haul down.

The gunfire stopped by Chloe's men who now approached Chloe surrounding Francisque who was on his knees with Chloe's gun pressed to his head.

"Likewise, but you really thought the Libya Islamic terrorist group would help you? Me and Rahman got a lot of history together."

"Let me guess you fucked him, too?"

"Of course, just like when I fucked you a while back in your younger days," she said.

"I had better," he said looking at Animal and Mayo who'd taken their masks off. "Let's see how better it is where you going."

"I'll let you know when I see you there," Francisque said before Chloe blew his brains out.

***

Port-Au-Prince, Haiti

Hours later the whole family was in their father/grandfather's mansion grieving over the loss of Francisque.

"How the fuck we let this happen, bro?" Boss asked Lil BD who was sitting in the living room looking at some old photos of Francisque when he was a kid.

"Don't beat yourself up, nephew. This is a part of life," Luc said walking into the living room with a gang of security guards.

"Yeah, but we just met him. You knew him your whole life and you don't seem to devastated," Lil BD stared Luc's brother Louis in the eye.

"I never cry over spilled milk, I take action. I'm as determined to find Chloe as y'all are."

"How do you know it was Chloe?" Luc said walking downstairs listening to every word Louis was saying and he sounded real fishy.

"Come on, Luc, it's clear as day. I hope you're not assuming I had anything to do with my father's death?" Louis shouted getting upset.

"No, I would never. I don't think you're that stupid, at least I hope not because if you was I would feed each body part to my baby sharks" Luc said seriously sitting down next to Lil BD.

Luc didn't feel like going back and forth so he walked out with his crew slamming the front door almost breaking it.

"After my father's funeral, we're going to hit the kill switch on Chloe because I believe she did kill my dad. When I was a kid Chloe and my dad used to fuck here and there but nothing serious he already knew what type of woman she was," Luc said.

"We ready," Boss said.

"Good, I gotta go make some calls," Luc said.

***

Two Weeks Later

Luc, Boss, and Lil BD sat in the front row of the funeral service listening to close friends of Francisque give speeches about how good of a person he was to anybody he came across.

Boss and Lil BD tried their best to listen to emotional friends and family speak their hearts, the only problem was the whole service was spoken in Creole.

"Y'all okay?" Luc asked.

"Yeah," Lil BD said watching the large group of Spanish men standing in the back behind the last row towards the exit door of the church.

"They good," Luc said, already seeing Mark and his goons paying respect to the fallen soldier.

Today was a long, sad day and Lil BD refused to get a close look at his grandfather's dead body. When he received the news of his father's murder weeks ago, he didn't give a fuck when Jenny told him. A while back Jenny and Lil BD were at a fast-food restaurant and she handed a homeless man a twenty-dollar bill because he was begging everyone for money.

When Lil BD told her that was his father she doubled back and gave him two hundred dollars. Jenny remembered his face so when she saw him on the news, she called him to tell him the bad news of his father's murder.

A couple of hours later the church cleared out and Mark and his goons approached Luc and his army who surrounded the church. Since his father's death he made sure security was extra tight. He couldn't afford any more losses.

"Luc, good to see you. The Santos Family sends our regards and respect to you and your family especially me and Hector," Mark said in his low pitched voice.

"Thank you for your support," Luc replied with Lil BD and Boss standing behind him.

"Your father was a very smart, honorable man. I'm sure you and your brother will carry on his legacy." Mark looked at the two young men behind him who didn't look Haitian at all.

"Thank you, be sure to tell your Uncle thanks for the concern and respect," Luc said.

"I will. Take care," Mark said, turning to leave.

Mark was a part of the Santos Cartel from Colombia. He was under his Uncle Hector a very powerful and wise man. Mark was thirty-four, healthy, had a family of his own, handsome, and a sneaky killer. He was the Santos Cartel mastermind he had numerous tactics that were unheard of.

"Something isn't right," Luc said watching Mark and his crew.

"What you mean?" Boss asked.

"It's a long story we have to go," Luc stated leaving the church.

Chapter 22

Nassau, The Bahamas

Louis arrived at the private island by a small boat to meet with one of the wealthiest men in the Caribbean. The beautiful, hot, tropical day was what Louis needed to put him in a good mood because lately, his life had been upside down. Since his father died it was like his brother had cut him off and kicked him out of the family because he believed he had a play in his father's death.

Louis loved his father dearly he was hurt when his brother tried accusing him of having anything to do with his dad's murder. He didn't go to his dad's funeral last week because he couldn't see him lying in a casket lifeless. Louis knew in life every soul lives and dies but to see the man who raised him was different.

The private walk-in beach had white sand leading to the glass beach house that was in front of him. In the front, he saw fruit trees and large waterfalls.

The guards led him inside the luxurious home to a private master wing where Maloney awaited his guest. Maloney was from the Freeport area of the Bahamas raised into a billionaire family. His family owned several Islands all over the world so when his parents died, he inherited all of their wealth and became one of the richest men in Central America and the Caribbean area.

Maloney was an older gentleman pushing the young age of fifty but he was fit and in shape because he was a swimmer. He was a white man with long, blonde dreadlocks and a caveman beard; he looked more like a white Rastafarian. He was a firm believer in the Shintoism religion founded in Japan. He was also a Martial arts expert, he trained all his guards who were now all just as deadly.

For decades Maloney supplied marijuana and heroin, but he only dealt with a few people mainly the European countries and the Costa Rica Cartel ran by a beautiful, young, dangerous woman who was only nineteen-years-old.

"Louis this visit is a surprise. When you called for a sit down I tried to figure out your agenda, but I found none whatsoever. Maybe you can bring light to this situation before I kill you," Maloney said, sitting in the middle of the large room floor Indian-style drinking tea.

"I came to speak business. I know you and my father have a history but I'm not him."

"History is not the type of word I would use. He killed my sister."

"And you killed my aunty two of them. So, I think we're all even," Louis replied looking into Maloney's blue eyes.

"What's your business proposal, Louis?"

"I need a heroin connection. My Brazil connect backed out for some reason. I have coke, you have dope and we can make millions together. Even though I'm sure you have plenty of money," Louis said.

"Why do you come to me when you could've gone somewhere else? You're a snake. How do I know your business will be a legit business?"

"I give you my word and I only snake those who snake me," Louis added.

"You know the best way to catch a snake?"

"No, I'm pretty sure you will tell me."

"While he or she is shedding or hunting their prey. And right now, your shedding. Your greed will one day be your downfall," predicted Maloney.

"You're a fortune teller now?"

"Somewhat, I just know a lot of things."

"Are you willing to do good business with me or not?"

"Sure, because I'm sure you heard the story about the two snakes in the pit?"

"No, I haven't."

"Good, I'll save that one for another day," Maloney said showing his vampire-like teeth.

***

Downtown Miami, FL

Hector was in his downtown condo sitting on his private, large, terrace watching the city traffic and civilians walking up and down the streets roller skating or on bikes.

Hearing the news of Francisque's death was shocking to him because he'd been in the game for a long time and was very connected all over the world especially in the United Kingdom area.

The two men had a long resume together; they used to do business together until things went left and the two families were in a deadly war for over ten years.

Both men eventually called a truce and stayed away from each other never crossing paths but both of them lost a lot in the war. He respected men like Francisque because he pushed a hard line and gave him a run for his money in the time of war.

Hector knew every boss had his day but there was so much crazy shit going on Hector was only worried about protecting his own.

Yesterday Mark told him RJ was found dead in his home garage and the Cuban Family was taking full responsibility for his death. He was happy about that, but RJ wasn't a threat it was Chloe and he swore to kill her slowly when he got his hands on her.

Hector has been married four times and one reason why was because Chloe killed his second wife while she was four months pregnant on her vacation to Mali. The Santos Cartel was the biggest family in Colombia but with Chloe out of the picture Columbia would be his.

***

Miami International Airport

Jenny got off her first-class flight happy to be off the plan, she hated planes after 9/11.

Lil BD told her to come to Miami days ago when he got back from Haiti because he wanted to spend time with her and make sure that she was safe. After all, Animal was still out lurking somewhere. Now she was pregnant, and he wanted her close by

The airport was jammed packed, Jenny called Lil BD to tell him she was tired and ready to get some shuteye.

***

Kylie grabbed her Louis Vuitton case from the luggage claim and made her way to the front of the airport. This was her second time in Miami, and she loved everything about it from the heat to the hurricane seasons.

Malik had been waiting for her to come down for a couple of days but she took care of her bills and her own apartment before leaving.

She wore a sundress and heels not trying to overdress but looking around all she saw were beautiful women in tight dresses, bikinis under booty shorts, and tops. One wore a see-through dress with thongs and no bra showing her saggy breasts.

Kylie made it outside to see a beautiful mixed woman she'd seen in Chicago standing there looking impatient. Kylie called Malik, he told her a limousine was on its way any second.

Jenny and Kylie stood outside until finally they see a long, white, stretch limousine pull up in front with dreads and guns on their hips.

"Jenny and Kylie?" one of the men asked.

Both said, "Yes!" Then looked at each other oddly.

"Lil BD and Malik are waiting for you both but first we're taking you both to the famous Dolphin Mall to go shopping. There is 250,000 apiece in both Goyard Bags in the back," he said, opening the door for them and shutting it as they both got inside.

"So, you're Malik's girl?" Jenny asked.

"Yeah."

"You're cute, I'm Jenny."

"Kylie, I don't really know what's going on but if one of them Haitians try something I got a pocket knife."

"Me too," Jenny said laughing, liking her already.

"No need for that, check your bags," one of the Haitians said after hearing their conversation.

Both of them pulled out handguns fully loaded.

"Perfect," Jenny said admiring the chrome Glock.

"I guess we're going shopping," Kylie said.

The two women talked, laughed, and joked all day enjoying each other's company.

Chapter 23

Key West, FL

Hitler gripped Candice's petite hips guiding her up and down on his dick while kissing her soft lips.

"Ahhh, yesss—mmmm—ohhh," she gasped and moaned.

She leaned back riding his dick, rocking her hips faster and faster trying to catch another orgasm experience. The bed was rocking back and forth as she thrust her hips lower making her ass clap on his dick making him hit her G-spot.

"Damn, baby," Hitler moaned, raising Candice and bringing her back down in slow motion, feeling her tight pussy wrap around his dick.

"Oh, my fucking God! Fuck me!" she screamed making her pussy squeeze around his dick, working her sex muscles and clenching for life on the dick.

"I'm cumminggg," she grunted trying to muffle her screams.

Her inner walls tightened, and her body locked while releasing her nut, she slid up on his wet dick before he came inside her. Candice got up panting heavily, dizzy, and trying to come back down from a different space and planet. She went and got a washcloth for herself and Hitler to clean themselves after over an hour and forty minutes.

Candice just stood there staring at him, naked, showing her sexy perfect body and big, plump pussy putting a gap between her thighs.

Candice had been seeing Hitler for weeks almost every day, she was feeling him hard. She brought him on her father's boat today just to spend time with him in private. She wasn't sexually active but when she felt his touch and the way he sucked her neck made her go crazy. Before she knew it, Candice was on her back with her legs in the air feeling Hitler dick pound her guts out.

"What's wrong?" Hitler said looking at her beautiful face walking toward him.

"Nothing I just want to know *what now?*"

"What do you mean? I'm fucking with you. I'm not going no-where."

"Just asking because I don't always give up the cookie so easy, it's just something about you."

"How many times you use that pick-up line?" he joked.

"I'm serious."

"How about we take a shower? Then you can go get your tan, while I cook dinner. And we head back to Miami to my place?" Hitler said kissing her lips.

"Sounds perfect," she said, getting up to go shower.

Hitler knew Candice was a good girl with a rich family. Home-girl had her own 225-foot Yacht and a beautiful condo. He'd been so focused on her he hadn't made no process on Boss's status which was his main reason for being down here.

This weekend he was hunting his prey, Miami was a big city, but Boss and Lil BD loved the limelight.

***

New York City, NY

Chloe was on the Upper Westside for fashion week. She loved Valentino and she knew the designer. He was from Colombia and he invited her to the Valentino show tonight. She looked amazing and lovely in a red land satin dress.

The place was filled with actors, designers, and wealthy people. Models cat-walked up and down the runway in the newest Valentino gear.

Due to so much going on in her life she needed a little getaway and what's not the best place to visit than New York? One of her favorite places in the world.

Chloe had been doing her research on Boss and the Haitian Mafia, they were somehow connected but she didn't know how. She knew Luc and his family didn't deal with outsiders, only family. As she sat there listening to Ne-Yo blur on the speakers a light bulb went off in her head, Janella was the connection to Boss and the Haitian Mafia.

Chloe had to get back to Colombia to figure out what Janella knew because she knew Janella played a part in this maze. She looked at her four big, muscle head goons letting them know she was ready to leave. Chloe stood to leave and walked out of the back exit. Two of her goons opened the backdoor escorting her out back of the kitchen area, to her limousine parked in the alleyway.

Boc! Boc! Boc! Boc! Boc! Boc! Boc! Boc! Boc!

Shots rang out from behind the dumpsters taking out both of Chloe's goons. The shooters killed Chloe's other two gunmen leaving her alone in the gun battle.

Boc! Boc! Boc! Boc! Boc!

Chloe hit one of the gunmen three times in the chest. Chloe couldn't see the other shooter, but she did see two vans flying into the alley. She saw eight gunmen hop out and start shooting at her. She ran all the way inside looking for another way out. The gunmen ran through the kitchen killing anybody who got in their way. Screams and cries could be heard all over the kitchen as gunfire took chunks out of the wall.

The gunmen saw Chloe running through the crowd of civilians watching the show and started shooting in her direction. People started running, yelling, ducking, and crawling around the place trying to escape the mayhem.

Chloe made it outside with people running out behind her like there was a bomb in the building. A cab was parked in front, Chloe jumped in the cab, yelling for him to pull off. When she was far away, she saw NYPD cops racing to the event.

***

Coconut Groove, Miami

"You think this shit gonna work?" Lil BD asked Malik who was sitting next to him in the large van that they'd stolen from a plumber's house in Carol City.

"It should, I saw it in a movie," Malik said looking at the nice brick house across the street with the manicured yard, drawing entrance, and new roof tile.

"How are we going to convince them to let us inside if they didn't call a plumbing service?" Lil BD said smelling the odor of his jumper he'd taken out of the back.

"Follow my lead I got this, bro," Malik said grabbing a snake tool to fix toilets and clean drains. While Lil BD grabbed the heavy toolbox.

Luc found out Chloe and Mayo were the ones who murdered his father. Francisque's pilot was an old Haitian man who was on the phone watching the gruesome murder of his fellow boss. The pilot heard Chloe called Mayo's name before leaving the crime scene, so the name stuck with him. He told Luc everything he saw and heard right before Luc killed him anyway just for being a coward, not fighting with his Haitian people and watching them die in pain.

Luc sent Lil BD and Malik to Mayo's parent's house to send a message in retaliation.

Mayo's parents were both in their early fifties and retired from working at banks all-across Miami. His family came from Peru to obtain a better life for their children but Mayo found his own way in life dealing with the Cartel. Mayo's grandmother also lived with his parents, was dying of cancer, and on her deathbed.

It was 9:00 a.m. and Mayo's parents were both preparing breakfast when the doorbell rang.

"Good morning, Ms. We're here going to house to house checking your water lines, pipes, and water systems because there was a big pipe burst a few blocks down causing a big flood in a few residential homes," Malik said looking at the old Spanish woman in her old lady gown.

"Ohhh, no, come in. We've actually been having a small issue with the kitchen drain," she said walking into the kitchen where her husband was. "These handsome young men came to help us fix the water system. They said it was a big accident down the street," she said.

"Okay, well let's let them do their job," The old man with a bald head and glasses said walking out the kitchen.

Lil BD pulled out his pistol and fired four shots into the old man's head. Malik followed up behind him, shooting his wife six times in the chest. Lil BD scanned the house and found an elder woman on her deathbed, plugged up to IVs and a breathing machine.

Boom!

He shot her in the face then left the room to find Malik standing at the door.

"Who was that?" Malik asked.

"Some old bitch already half-dead," Lil BD said leaving the murder scene thinking about Jenny and how she was starting to show in her pregnancy.

Romell Tukes

Chapter 24

Months Later

Colombia, Bogota

Chloe walked through the tunnel on her way to see Janella to try to put everything together. For the past couple of months, Chloe had been stuck in New York for safety reasons. She found out the Cuban Cartel was behind the hit at the Valentino fashion show. She knew the Cubans had very strong ties to New York so she chose to lay low for a while before coming back to Colombia. She'd been doing a lot of thinking and trying to figure out Boss and Luc's affiliation, but she couldn't put the connection together.

Chloe saw Janella eating a peanut and jelly sandwich with two guards on watch duty because they were accountable for her. If anything was to go wrong, Chloe would have their heads on a plate.

"Janella, how are my men treating you?" Chloe said pulling up a chair next to her bed.

"Fair."

"Good, good! I'm trying to get you some better food. But do you know this man, Janella?" Chloe said, handing her a pic of Francisque.

"I'm sorry, I don't," Janella lied sternly in an unenthused tone.

Chloe looked at her with an enticing smile. "Well, he was recently murdered. Me and him used to be something like a couple. So, I just want to find his killers," she said, noticing that Janella wasn't biting the bait.

"I'm sorry to hear that wish I could help," Janella said, passing her the photobook as far as her chairs could reach.

"Thanks anyway, but here go another picture just in case you couldn't really see," Chloe said, handing her Francisque's funeral service picture of his born and death date with a *Rest In Peace* sign above his picture.

When Janella saw the paper of her father's death tears filled her eyes. The whole time she thought Chloe was lying trying to gain information of some type out of her about her father.

"Who is he to you?" Chloe said realizing that she'd hit a nerve.

"I don't know him," Janella said with tears.

"Okay, have it your way. But I'ma kill you just like I did him," Chloe said with a monstrous look before standing up to leave.

Janella couldn't believe Chloe had figured out who her father was. *But how?* She thought while mourning over his death. Janella had to find a way out or she would kill her kids next. When Chloe said she was fucking her dad she wondered if that's what all this was about.

***

Miami, FL

Days Later

"Mayo, I'm sorry about what happened to your family. I had no clue this would transgress this far," Chloe said sitting at a bar owned by Victor.

"It's all part of life, but I won't stop until I kill Francisque's whole family," he stated with assuredness in his voice.

"I'm with you but our main targets are Boss and Luc. I'm still trying to figure out how to surmise their ties. I don't believe Boss is Haitian he's from Chicago for crying out loud."

"Luc is the one we have to worry about. I told you killing his father would start some big shit. Victor was against at first until I convinced him."

"That's why I love you, Mayo, but give it some time. They will pop up."

"I know, if not I have no problem going hunting, they're in my city. Did you get the shipment my people sent to Chicago the other day?"

"Yes, thank you. Everything is moving at a rapid pace the city loves it," Chloe said drinking a glass of Champagne Moet.

"I just want to evaluate something just because we're in business together and I'm in the battlefield doesn't mean I trust you. Because I won't hesitate to kill you if you cross any line, beautiful," Mayo said before leaving with his men who were waiting on him outside the empty bar.

"Why everybody always treats me like the bad guy in life," she said out loud.

"Because Chloe, you're the devil in make-up!" Mayo yelled back hearing her comment while on his way out the door.

***

North Miami, FL

Lexus was cleaning her condo while preparing a meal for her man and father who were on his way over for dinner. Tonight was a nervous night for Lexus because she planned to introduce Boss to her dad.

She'd never presented any man to her dad because she never loved any man or wanted to spend her life with someone as much as she did with Boss. Last week she graduated from college, so she spent most of her time with Boss.

He even moved in with her after she forced him to, but he was never really there. She knew he lived a lifestyle that was spent a lot of time in the street.

Lexus was deeply in love with Boss every time she looked at him her heart would melt like butter in a hot pan.

"How do I look, baby?" Boss said coming out of the backroom in a black Tom Ford's suit with a big face GMT Master Rolex watch and a GIA certified bracelet with diamond-encrusted 18K.

"Handsome and legit which is perfect. My father owns a chain of businesses so when you tell him you own a car dealership in Chicago he will be, please. Also, tell him you plan to open one up out here," she said nervously.

"Babe, relax I got this," Boss said as the doorbell rang.

Lexus fixed her dress, kissed him on his lip, and went to let her dad in. Boss knew this day would come but he had plans to speak to her father one on one because he was in love with Lexus and she was the woman he planned to be with forever.

"Ty, this is my father and his wife," Lexus said nervously, acting fidgety.

Boss saw an older Spanish man in a suit with a serious look and a beautiful young wife who was shaped like a coke bottle.

"Pleased to meet you, sir. Lexus has told me a lot about you," Boss said extending his hand, Lexus's father shook his hand firmly.

"I've heard a little about you, Ty. Also nice to meet you. How about you two beautiful women prepare dinner while me and Ty go talk," he told his wife and daughter.

"Okay, daddy, love you and be nice," Lexus said seriously, giving him the evil eye.

Once on the private balcony, Lexus's father looked Boss up and down checking his attire approving of his style.

"What do you do for a living, Ty?"

"I own a car dealership in Chicago and I plan to open one down here soon, sir."

"Please don't call me, sir. Not when you're fucking my daughter. Now I want to be clear, I love my daughter and she speaks very highly of you. If you hurt her, you hurt me and that won't be good. Do I make myself clear?"

"Yes," Boss said, looking in his eyes with no fear.

"What's your plans in life?"

"That's what I wanted to talk to you about. I grew up in poverty in Chicago rough streets. I made mistakes, but I grew from them all. I became a man and an entrepreneur. I undertake success. I only ever loved two women in my life, and one is my mother. I never felt the way I feel about your daughter with no other woman. Life is short and with your permission, I would love to marry your daughter?" Boss said, seeing the shocked expression on his face.

"Are you sure you're willing to give yourself to one woman, son? Marriage isn't as fun as it sounds."

"I will do whatever I have to do to keep her in my life. I respect you for raising a good strong woman and with your grace and blessing, I will protect her and give her everything she deserves," Boss said, looking at him staring into the clouds.

"Does she know you want to marry her?"

"No."

"When do you plan on asking her?"

"Whenever I receive your blessing," Boss added.

"What are you waiting for?"

"Lexus!" Boss yelled watching her dad move to the side.

Lexus came out thinking something was wrong but when she saw Boss get on one knee, she lost it.

"Lexus, will you marry me, baby. I want to spend the rest of my life with you," Boss said, pulling out a box with a round, brilliant diamond 5.41 cart, 2 baguettes, four triangular diamonds worth 1.9 1/2 million dollars.

"Yesssss! Oh, my God, Ty. I can't believe you," Lexus said on her knees crying.

Her father smiled while holding his wife and watching young love.

"I'm paying for the wedding. Now, let's go eat, y'all making me hungry," Lexus father said.

Romell Tukes

Chapter 25

Orchid Island, FL

Lexus looked in the mirror almost ready to cry again but she was scared to mess up her make-up she'd just applied. Today was her big day and she felt like she couldn't breathe, she was a nervous wreck dealing with her anxiety. When Boss asked her to marry him it was as if he'd read her mind. That was two months ago and today she was ready to give herself to him in marriage. She already knew about his last marriage and the death of his ex-wife, but she didn't give a fuck he was the man of her dreams.

Her father owned a beach house mansion, so she wanted to throw her wedding day on a beach and then take a cruise for her honeymoon. Boss friends planned to attend the honeymoon but the 681-foot boat had four different sections so they may never see each other.

Lexus wore an all-white long Geline dress with Tiffany and Company jewelry around her neck worth 4.6 million dollars she had for years but never wore.

"How's the bride-to-be? It's almost time, baby. All the guests are seated, your husband is out there, and the DJ is ready to play your favorite Selena song," her father said admiring his beautiful daughter.

"Thank you for everything, daddy, you're the best," she said holding back her emotions.

"You never have to thank me, baby. You're my everything, all I ask is when I die you take over the family business. You're all I got," her father said fixing his tuxedo blazer.

"Father, we already talked about that. You know I'm not built for that type of stuff," Lexus said looking up at her father's eyes.

"Baby, you're a Santos. No matter how many times you change your name," her father said strongly.

"I know father it's in my blood."

"Yes, it is, baby girl. Now let's get you married," Hector Santos said, proud of his little girl.

***

Boss stood on the small stage looking over the large crowd of four hundred guests, mostly Spanish people. Lil BD and Malik were his best men; they stood to the left of him.

Lexus made the grand entrance out the back of the mansion, down the stairs, leading onto a platform made just for her so she wouldn't have to walk in the sand. The Selena music played loud while everybody watched Lexus walk down the long aisle with her father by her side. Everybody was amazed at how astonishing she looked.

Once the couple was face to face neither one of them could stop smiling. The Catholic Priest gave his speech in English and Spanish. Boss wanted a Muslim Islamic wedding, but Lexus was Catholic and so was her whole family, so he gave in. He tried to have her convert to Islam, but she said it wasn't in her heart yet because the only religion she knew was Catholic.

After they said their vows and kissed it was official. Lexus sported the huge rock on her finger and tossed her flowers in the air. Jenny caught them and winked at Lil BD who was already her husband.

Hector introduced Boss and Lexus to some powerful people from all over the world who came out to show respect to the Cartel leader daughter.

There was a big dinner party inside the beautiful mansion for the newlyweds and family and friends. The boat arrived close to midnight and the three couples made their way on board. Boss, Lexus, Lil BD, Jenny, Malik, and Kylie were ready for the cruise they had to themselves.

"This boat is huge," Kylie said walking down the long hall-ways.

"This shit is fly, Boss. But we're going to the other side," Lil BD said, taking Jenny the opposite way to find a big, nice room to cuddle in.

"A'ight good night, bro. We'll see y'all for breakfast. I have no clue where the dining area is at but we'll just all meet up here. Me and Lexus are going upstairs," Boss said and everybody agreed and went different ways.

There were forty-two rooms on the boat, four pool areas, a tennis and basketball court, a gym, six bars with bartenders, eight gourmet chefs, and three levels.

"You want to go to the bar, baby?" Boss asked his wife.

"No, we've had enough to drink, let's go to the room," she said, grabbing his dick kissing him.

"Lead the way," Boss said, following her up three flights of stairs.

Once inside the master room, it looked like a small condo with a kitchen, living room, terrace, Jacuzzi, high ceilings, and three rooms with French doors.

Lexus went into the first room which was all white with fur rugs and a fireplace. She took off her wedding dress and Boss undid his clothes sitting on the bed.

"You look so perfect," he said looking at her flawless body while she seductively sashayed toward him before getting on her knees and taking his hard dick down her throat.

She went down on his dick with her warm mouth and wet tongue sucking the skin off his dick.

"Shitttt, Lexus," he moaned.

She was sucking at a fast pace banging his cock down her throat with no gag reflex like a white girl. He exploded in her mouth while she still sucked up and down slowly swallowing everything.

Boss tossed her on the bed onto her stomach and slid his dick down her ass crack, stopping at her tiny brown hole. Boss then stopped and buried his face into her ass cheeks eating her ass.

"Ohhh, Bosss, yesss! Eat that ass!" she yelled and gripped the pillows in front of her. After a couple of minutes of eating her ass, he slid his dick into her ass hole.

Lexus's body tensed up when his dick slid in and out her ass. "Uggghhh," she moaned trying to run but he pinned her down and tore her ass up.

Lexus's screams of pleasure could be heard down the hall. She climaxed out of her ass and pussy making her want more. She rode his dick while he stretched her ass hole loving how it felt before he came in his wife and they switch positions to missionary. The sex landed them all over the place as they explored each other bodies.

***

Malik had Kylie in the glass shower bent over with her handprints all over the window.

"Ohhh, Malik, fuck me harder!" Kylie yelled feeling him in her stomach.

Malik spread her cheeks wider and went deeper into the slippery pussy.

"Don't move, bitch," he said, talking dirty the way she liked.

He lifted her right leg up and choked her lightly slamming angrily into her making her go crazy hitting all her spots. Malik gave her deep strokes until they climaxed in the shower. Once out of the shower, they continued their lovemaking in the lesson to some soft R&B.

***

Lil BD had Jenny cuffed up to the bed ass naked using his tongue to seduce her, trailing up her upper thighs until he made it to the thin, perfect pussy lips. He eats her pussy like a pro.

"Uhhhmmm," she moaned while he sucked her clit until she climaxed quickly.

Lil BD then put his dick into her wetness feeling her pussy walls attach his dick in a chokehold. He made love to her slowly while listening to Usher on surround sound. Her pussy was wet and at its best, because she was pregnant. They made love until they couldn't go no more.

Chapter 26

Santiago, DR

Luc's wife was taking a bubble bath and listening to music while her kids were asleep finally because they'd had her up all day running around crazy like a chicken with her head cut off.

It was hard being a full-time mom, raising two daughters alone because Luc was only home twice a month if that. She knew he had a family to run especially with his father gone but she still needed him to be a father.

Lela listened to the new Becky G album, sliding her index finger in her pussy going in a circular motion thinking about Luc the only man she desired.

She thought she'd heard a loud noise, she stood up with soap all over her body to turn down the music and two big Spanish men in suits busted into her bathroom. She screamed and slipped back into the tub.

"This is a nice view, I love my Dominican women," Mayo said walking into the bathroom.

"What do you want?" she asked, covering her breasts.

"Luc, you, the kids, and whoever else I can get my hands on. Revenge is the sweetest thing next to pussy. I believe 2 Pac said that?" Mayo said looking at his guards for confirmation.

"Please don't touch my daughters, they have nothing to do with this, take me," she said trembling.

"Too late," Mayo said, whistling for his goons to show her the surprise.

When Lela saw her two daughters being dragged into the room by their hair she wanted to cry.

"Please you're going to hurt them", Lela said, seeing blood leak in a trail. When the guards lifted the little girl's beautiful faces, both of their necks were slit wide open. "Ahhh, nooo!" she yelled crying in tears.

Mayo closed his ears, this was the part of killing he hated, the loud cries, begging, and pleas.

"Are you done? You sure know how to ruin a surprise," Mayo told one of his goons before putting his attention back on Lela." So, where is Luc?"

"Fuck you."

"She is a very pretty girl," Mayo told his guards. He grabbed Lela's hair, choking her then drowning her for twenty more seconds. "How about you tell me now?"

"Fuck you, bitch," she spat taking breaths before he drowned her for twenty more seconds.

"Have it your way," Mayo said looking at the stereo next to the tub." Becky G, huh?" he said listening to her sing.

Lela closed her eyes because she could read the expression on his face.

Mayo pushed the stereo into the tub water killing her from the powerful electric shocks.

***

Golden Beach, FL

"Hector, I've been working extra hard night and day trying to figure this shit out."

"How many times will you tell me the same news? I feel as if you're a waste of money and fresh air," Hector said to his private investigator.

"Sir, I have been doing this type of work for over thirty years and Chloe moves as if she knows someone is following her," The P.I said sitting in Hector's office.

"Joe, how hard can it be to keep an eye on a chick who barely does nothing when she is in my city?" Hector asked the white ex-cop who he paid one million dollars to, to find an accurate location on Chloe.

"I know she is having issues with more than one family. I was in New York at the fashion show when the Cubans almost killed her, but I believe she is plotting on something or someone, sir," Joe said.

"That's all you got for me? Shit, I already knew all this, Joe. I'm sorry but your time is up, I'll find someone else."

"Do I get to keep the money?"

"Of course, you can." Hector pulled out a golden Glock 9mm from his desk and fired two shots in Joe's left eye.

Four guards came into his office, snatched Joe's body out of the chair, and dragged him out the room.

"Don't get no blood on my floor. That's why I shot him in the eye!" Hector yelled before putting on his reading glasses and continued his newspaper.

***

South Miami, FL

Days Later

Boss was driving an all-black Wraith to Lil Haiti for a meeting with Luc. Last week Luc told them Mayo killed his family and he was crushed about that.

Luc had cameras in his mansion and two guards who were there 24/7 but they were killed also by Mayo and his team. When Luc watched the cameras, he was sick at the way his enemy sliced his daughter's necks in their beds.

"Pull over at McDonald's, bro, I'm starving," Lil BD said seeing a McDonalds on the corner

"Damn, nigga you just ate an hour ago. You sure you, not the one pregnant?" Boss joked.

"Come on with the jokes but that cruise was popping, bro. The jet skis were the best until that big ass shark tried to get at Malik. You saw how scared that niggas was?" Lil BD said laughing.

"Facts I was crying," Boss said, pulling into the busy fast-food restaurant.

"You want something?"

"Nah, but I gotta come in and take a piss," Boss said, placing his gun in his waist before getting out.

135

Boss and Lil BD walked into the fast-food spot seeing that it was a little kid's birthday party. As Lil BD went to order his food, he ran into little Spanish kids everywhere.

"Can I get a number four?"

"Excuse me, sir, but it's noon. Breakfast is over," a black chick said rudely.

"So why the fuck is breakfast still up?"

"Because maybe if your funny looking ass ain't rush to my register I coulda changed it," she said snapping her neck like a true hoodrat tapping her long, hook nails on the counter.

"What? Bitch—you better watch your fucking mouth before I slap the black off your gums," Lil BD spat back getting fired up.

"Nigga, you not doing shit to me that's on everything. I'll have my brother and them Park projects niggas down in seconds on your ass!" she shouted.

Boss heard the loud commotion as he was coming out of the bathroom. When he saw Lil BD's face, he knew he had to get him before someone got hurt.

"We out, come on," Boss said, grabbing Lil BD who was still yelling and talking shit.

Stepping outside Boss saw the familiar face rushing toward them. Boss pushed Lil BD to the ground and pulled out his gun busting at Hitler who was too late and catching a bullet in his shoulder.

Bloc! Bloc! Bloc! Bloc! Bloc! Bloc! Bloc!

Boom! Boom! Boom!

Hitler shot back while trying to duck behind a delivery van. Hitler was stopping at McDonald's to grab a milkshake before he went to meet Candice at her college. When he saw Lil BD inside, he waited for him to come out, and seeing Boss was a two for one special but he didn't expect him to be strapped.

The shootout lasted two minutes until both parties heard sirens at a distance and ran to their cars getting away from the scene. Unaware that two civilians had been killed in broad daylight.

"We could have had that nigga. I can't believe that bitch nigga tried to kill me," Lil BD said.

"How he know we was down here?"

"I told him, I thought he was going to ride."

"Guess not," Boss said entering the Little Haiti area.

Romell Tukes

Chapter 27

Nassau, Bahamas

Louis was on the boat with three of his guards looking into the ocean on his way to see Maloney who asked him to come for an emergency meeting.

In the past couple of months, Louis had been busy traveling the world on business affairs. He had so many deals with big-name powerful families.

A lot of Cartel families didn't deal with the Haitian Mafia because of Francisque for many reasons but most had feared him or had a longtime beef with him.

Louis took it upon himself to fill those gaps and build new trust and business bonds with families his father always told him to stay away from.

Three weeks ago, Maloney sent him a couple of tons of pure dope in exchange for coke. When Louis got the dope, he sold it all to his people in Gator and they paid top dollar for the best heroin they'd ever received.

Once on Maloney's island, Louis' goons were told to stay on the boat while Maloney's five-man team of trained assassins walked him inside to their boss.

***

Maloney was sitting in a chair eating a fruit salad surrounded by an entourage.

"Louis thanks for coming out. I'm very sorry for the short notice. I know you're a busy man, have a seat."

Louis took a seat and took off his blazer because the room was a little hot as if he didn't own an AC.

"What's going on big dog?" Louis said watching Maloney lick his fingers then wipe his mouth with a napkin.

"It's people like you Louis that make blacks look bad. That's why nobody with any common sense would trust a black man."

"I'm not black, I'm Haitian."

"Whatever you call it and I'm Jesus," he said, making a couple of his guard's laugh.

"What is this about?"

"Oh, you don't know? How fatuous and asinine can you fucking be Louis? The coke you sent to Trinidad was stolen and whoever stole it killed six of my best men!" Maloney shouted angrily.

Louis was silent, he had no clue his shipment had been hijacked, this made him look bad. Maloney's goons all draw their weapons on him.

"You better start talking, I'll give you two minutes to spare your life," Maloney said while finishing his fruit salad.

"Maloney, I'm so sorry about this. I swear on my father's grave. I had no parts in this. You have to believe me. Let me make this shit right. My family and the Trinidad Mafia been rivals forever, but I had no clue they would disrespect me like that. Sending the coke to Trinidad was the only way I could get the coke to you. I promise I will repay you everything that was stolen," Louis said with fear in his eyes looking around at all the guns pointed at him.

Maloney looked at Louis with his cold, blue eyes and told his goons to lower their guns. "The only reason why you're not dead is because I know how the Trinidad Mafia get down and the history you and your family have with them. Next time send the shipment to Barbados those are my people. If this happens again, I won't have a sit down with you," Maloney warned sternly.

"I understand, thank you. I'ma take care of it."

"Good, you can leave. I left you a gift outside as a token of our friendship," Maloney said before Louis was led out by his goons.

Outside Louis took a deep breath as he got back on the boat thinking about what the Trinidad Mafia did. He had to go see Luc today to straighten this shit out because he was the only one who could. Louis saw his security guards all dead with headshots stacked up on top of each other in a pile. Louis was upset but he knew Maloney did it for the loss of his men so Louis respected the game.

***

Miami Beach, FL

Chloe grabbed her purse, leaving her mansion on her way to meet Victor to explain to him everything that was going on and who was setting her up and why.

It took her months to put everything together but she did her research with the help of a young computer hacker from Dade County. She found out that Janella was born in Haiti and was the daughter of Francisque and that meant her two sons were his grandson. If she would've known everything led back to Janella, she would've never kidnapped her, but she'd taken her for her own personal reasons. She had no clue a schoolteacher would be the daughter of one of the most powerful men in the world.

She walked down her spiral glass staircase where her team of eight awaited her. Since the beef, she rolled with an eight-man team with high power weapons just in case.

They filled up two black SUVs driving away from the estate. The community was in a gated establishment with a security booth near the gates to make sure the wealthy resident was safe and comfortable. Residences, family, and friends had to get confirmed before entering the richest area in Miami.

The SUVs pulled out of the gates, and they saw four minivans about to past them. When the vans crossed lines into their path, the passengers in the SUVs got into panic mode.

Twenty Cubans jumped out firing assault rifles at the SUV. Chloe and her goons rushed out to engage in the gun battle. Chloe hit two Cubans with clean headshots while four goons covered her.

Boc! Boc! Boc! Boc!

Tat! Tat! Tat! Tat! Tat!

Two more of the Cubans dropped from Chloe rounds but only two of her men were left standing.

"Boss go through the woods, it's many of them," one of the guards said, thinking she was still behind him, but she was already dashing through the woods. Chloe knew when to fold her cards and right now was a primary example.

The Cubans surrounded her two goons left standing killing them but seeing no Chloe.

"Bitch!" Mark yelled looking into the woods knowing she'd escaped again.

***

North Miami, FL

Hector's wife Allison was getting undress preparing for her weekly massage at a new massage parlor. She'd spent a lot of time pampering her beauty and body. Allison was a thirty-one-year-old Colombian woman who came from poverty until she met Hector. He gave her a new life ten years ago and she loved him for that.

Her beauty was pure without make-up and her body stopped traffic everywhere she went. She had big titties, a phat ass with wide hips to match, and thick thighs.

She laid down on the table and placed her small face in the rest relaxing her body. She always preferred males mainly black to do her body treatment because they were stronger and handier than women.

The door opened and a man walked inside. He wasted no time in pouring oil on her back and rubbing her inner back softly.

"Harder," she said.

He went harder digging his elbows into her back but more painful than the women did.

"You're going too hard. Oh my God, you're, okay," she said lifting her head to see Mayo with a gun at her face.

Psst! Psst! Psst! Psst!

He took the silencer off his pistol and walked out leaving her bleeding all over the floor.

Chapter 28

Two Months Later

Dade County, FL

Jenny was in Dade County Hospital giving birth, her water had broken hours ago while she was on her way home with Lil BD coming from a lunch date.

Lil BD was calling Boss on speaker while the Cuban doctor was telling Jenny to push harder when he felt the little boy's head trying to force his way out.

"Bro, come to the hospital it's coming out hurry," Lil BD said looking at Jenny's face which showed that she was in pain as sweat dripped down her face.

The baby was supposed to be due in a month but her body said differently today.

"I'm downstairs, nigga," Boss said through the phone.

Lil BD hung up and began helping Jenny, giving her words of encouragement. She told him to shut up while she pushed like a madwoman and held on to the bed rails like she was about to snatch them off.

Lil BD saw Boss standing outside the window with Luc and his goons because he was the only one that was allowed in the room.

When the baby finally came out, Jenny and Lil BD both had tears of joy. They'd delivered a handsome 7 ½ pound baby boy with bright hazel eyes, light skin, and deep dimples.

Lil BD walked outside the room surrounded by Haitians and his family.

"You're a father now, bro," Boss said, hugging him.

"Congratulations, nephew," Luc said, handing him a Cuban cigar. Remembering when his daughters were born brought a wave of emotion over him.

"Thank you," he said looking at Jenny holding his son making him feel ten times more of a man.

***

Days Later

Summerland Key, FL

Hector walked into the 24,719 square foot mansion with two of his personal bodyguards. The mansion belonged to the Mayor of Miami who was a good friend of Hector for a very long time.

The Mayor was throwing a big party tonight for his sixty birthday and everybody came out to show support. Hector wasn't going to come out, but the Mayor always showed him love and he did a lot for the Santos Family.

Hector took a glass of Don P from one of the waiters and stood looking at all the beautiful women around, dancing to the soft jazz and talking to whoever would listen. Since the death of his wife, he'd been lying low until he came up with a solid plan but he knew who was responsible.

"Hector my friend," the mayor said, approaching Hector with two beautiful young Spanish women behind him.

"Johnny, happy birthday. I don't know how you do it? You don't look a year over twenty," Hector said embracing him as they shared laughs.

"If I tell you my secret, I may have to kill you," he told Hector in his ear.

"Some secrets are to die for," Hector replied.

"I have to go upstairs and take care of something. Enjoy your night," the Mayor said, walking off with the two women on his arms.

Hector's stomach started to bubble making him fart in public unable to control himself.

"I have to go take a shit, let's find a restroom," Hector told his men. They found a restroom down the hall away from the party scene.

Both of his guards stood outside of the bathroom door watching two waiters with trays walk down the hallway.

"Excuse me but this bathroom is occupied," one of the guards said to both of the men who must have had to use the bathroom.

Luc swiftly pulled out a long switchblade that he had tied into his dreads. Malik saw both bodyguard's necks split open with one swing from Luc as he looked at him like he was crazy.

It didn't long for the guards to drop in very slow motion. "Grab them and put them in the closet, I got Hector," Luc said, opening the bathroom door.

***

Hector was on the toilet shitting non-stop. Little did he know the Don P Malik served him had Laxative tablets in it so he could fall into their trap.

Luc walked around the corner in the large walk-in bathroom to see Hector holding the wall taking a shit.

"Hector, good to see you," Luc said, scaring him and catching him with his pants down.

"Luc, what a surprise. Wrong time wrong place, I guess," Hector said.

"You can say that, but I just got to you before you got to me. I remember when I was a little kid your men ran into my house and killed my mother. My brother and sister's mother had to raise me as her own with my dad. I never forgot your face or voice. I was hiding in the closet the whole time. That day you turned me into a real killer, so thank you," Luc said, pulling out a P89 Roger with a long silencer attached to it.

"About time, you were starting to bore me with your sorrow story. People die every day, kid," Hector said before Luc fired seven shots into his head leaving him slumped on the toilet.

Luc walked out, and Malik was standing there on point watching the party.

"Time to go," Luc said, leading the way out the side door.

***

Downtown Miami

Julianne sat in the back of a bookstore reading a hood novel called, *Murda Season* by a new hot author named Romell Tukes. Her bodyguards waited outside for her like she demanded. Julianne was sexy, tall, and curvy, with green eyes, curly short hair, and a fit, toned body from years of running track. She was Peruvian and the daughter of Victor. She was a party girl but also about her business. When her father or Mayo wasn't around or busy with other things she would run the operations.

She heard someone clear their throat standing in front of her. "You're fucking late, sit down," she said to her guest she'd been waiting on.

"You look beautiful."

"Cut the bullshit. What do you want, Louis? And sorry about what happened to your father," she said.

"How are you sorry when your people did it?" Louis asked.

"Chloe is not our people. My family only does business with her. I don't know why she may be fucking them and the whole security team, who knows?" she said.

"Whatever, but I need a favor from you?"

"Oh, hell no, papi. Your favors come with a death wish," Julianne said

"I need ecstasy, a few pounds."

"That's all?"

"No, I also need a couple of tons of coke."

"Louis you sell coke. Why do you need coke?"

"A hurricane wiped out everything I had in Haiti."

"Nigga what hurricane, it's July?"

"Julianne, can you please just do it? Please I need you. I would never ask you if it wasn't important."

"I'll think about it and contact you, but this is the last time. If my father finds out I'm having any dealings with his enemy we're both dead," she said grabbing her Louis Vuitton bag.

"Thank you, I know you still love me," Louis said.

"You wish, that was years ago," she said leaving.

Chapter 29

Ibague, Colombia

Chloe's mother was an elder, eighty-year-old woman with a lot of health problems and loss of memory but Chloe had seven guards and nurses watching over her 24/7. She lived on a small ranch with six acres of land full of horses and cows. Chloe's mom normally laid in the bed during the day and night watching old Spanish movies from the 60s and 70s.

Two guards were on the front porch enjoying the nice evening view. They saw two women driving up the dirt road on small motorcycles with flower baskets in the front of the handlebars. The men stood up watching the two beautiful women climb off the bikes with long hair, long, nice legs, and attractive bodies.

"Flowers," Kylie said in English.

"How much?" one of the guards asked.

Jenny and Kylie looked at each and laughed signaling their que.

Boc! Boc! Boc! Boc! Boc!

The women killed both men before running onto the porch hiding on both sides of the door.

"I'll take the first," Jenny said, hearing running footsteps in the house.

The door flew open and a big Spanish man ran out with a gun clutched in his right hand.

Boc! Boc! Boc!

Jenny shot him in the head, then kicked his dead body down the stairs while Kylie entered the house.

Kylie saw a shooter coming down the stairs with an AR assault rifle but before he had a chance to pull the trigger she fired two rounds into his chest and his body rolled down the stairs.

"Nice shoot," Jenny said.

"Thank you, I been at the range with Malik but I like the bigger guns, I feel a—" Kylie words were cut short by a gunman letting off shots from the kitchen.

Tat! Tat! Tat! Tat! Tat! Tat! Tat!

Jenny and Kylie both hid behind the wall dodging the hail of bullets. Jenny saw an entrance to the kitchen through the living room area while the gunman continued to shoot. Jenny crept up behind the young Colombia shooter who looked no older than seventeen.

Boc! Boc! Boc! Boc!

Jenny splattered his brains all over the kitchen walls making a big mess.

"There's gotta be more of them," Jenny said hearing the floor screech above her. "Upstairs," Jenny said and they made their way up the wooden staircase.

Both women heard loud music coming from a room to their left, it sounded like the type of music that Mexicans played at a bar. Jenny and Kylie slowly opened the door with the gun locked and loaded in front of them but what they saw next disgusted them.

Two Spanish men were ass naked having rough sex with the old Spanish woman who looked like she didn't have a clue what was going on.

One man had his dick in her pussy and the other man fucked her in her ass from behind her. Chloe's mom was taking the dick like a champ, with her long saggy titties flopping everywhere.

Boc! Boc! Boc! Boc! Boc!

"Ahhh—"

Boc! Boc! Boc! Boc!

Chloe's mom's body rolled off the bed and she tried crawling under the bed. Jenny couldn't help but laugh before Kylie emptied the clip in her old fragile body.

"Yeah, I love this shit!" Kylie cheered,

"I think you need help. Can we go now, please?" Jenny said walking out of the room.

***

Coconut Grove, Miami

Luc had a small house in the suburbs that he rarely used until recently after his family was killed but he liked quiet areas, he could get a piece of mind. Today he was in his backyard barbecuing with Boss, he loved cooking on his grill when he had time to.

"How's the married life nephew? You already got bags under your eyes," Luc said, lifting the grill to check on the grilled chicken, fish, steak, and goat.

"Lexus's father was killed last week, so she's been crying, exhausted, and planning for his funeral arrangements. She told me she was about to take over his business because she had no choice. I think he owns some big business because his money up," Boss said sitting in a lawn chair drinking a beer.

"Sorry to hear that but this is the time she needs you the most. So, just make sure you're there for her," Luc said seriously.

"Facts."

"What's his name anyway?" Luc asked, flipping over slobs of steak.

"Lexus's last name was Santos, but I heard people call him, Mr. H," Boss said.

"Wait, wait, wait—Lexus's last name is Santos?"

"Yeah, why?" Boss said thinking back to when his grandfather mentioned the Santos Cartel.

"Wait right here," Luc said, rushing into the house hoping this wasn't what he thought was because if it was they had a big problem on their hand.

Luc came back out with a photo of Hector and passed it to Boss.

"That's her father," Boss said.

"Fuck!" Luc screamed.

"What's going on, Luc? I'm a little confused."

"Boss, I killed Santos because he killed my mother years ago."

"What? I thought you and my mom had the same mother and father?"

"No, I had a different mother. She was murdered by Santos when he was beefing with my father. Me and Malik took him out at the Mayor's party that I knew he attended every year. You remember at my father's funeral? The Colombians that came were Hector's people making sure my father was really dead. They had plans to break the truce and attack, so I attacked first. I know how they get down."

"Damn, so this means Lexus is taking over his Cartel?"

"Yeah, this could go both ways but if she finds out you have dealings with the people who killed her father. You could be in serious danger, nephew. If she is anything like her father or Mark, then you may have to sleep with one eye open," Luc joked but was very serious.

"This is some crazy shit," Boss said, wondering why Lexus never told him her father was a Cartel boss.

He should've seen the signs. Lexus told him many times her father was a powerful man. Boss was at a loss of thoughts this was the first time he didn't know what to do.

***

North Miami, FL

Torres stepped out of his apartment early in the morning right before sunrise in a white lab coat, carrying a suitcase. This was Torres's everyday routine, he moved like he had a real nine-to-five job. He climbed in his Benz c-class pulling out his parking spot on his way across town.

Animal put the Hellcat in drive to follow him at a good distance, he'd been tailing Torres for a couple of weeks. He had been up for days, he'd prolonged inability to obtain adequate sleep since he'd been stalking Torres.

Twenty minutes later, Animal saw Torres enter the same old morgue he'd been coming to every morning since he'd been tailing him.

Once Torres was inside Animal grabbed his gun, pulled his hoodie over his head, and walked across the street.

Inside the empty building which looked like a mini-hospital, Animal opened the double doors leading down a long hallway that looked like it never ended.

Animal saw a lot of empty rooms with glass windows. When he made it halfway down the hall he saw Torres in the windows with his back toward him doing something, but it was really hard to see what exactly he was doing.

When Animal walked into the room, Torres handed him a letter that read: *I know you've been following me. But when you come inside please be quiet and don't disturb me until I'm done, thank you.*

When Animal was done reading Torres's letter, he knew he wasn't stable. He walked into the room, Animal smelled a strong odor of death, a smell he was used to by now.

Torres paid him no mind while continuing to work on his masterpiece.

Animal saw two dead Spanish women laying on the tables, one was a teenager. The other woman was in her early 30s from the looks of her mature body.

Animal watched Torres cut into the older woman's stomach then dig into her tissue for something. Animal saw another letter on the empty table which read,

This is my daughter and wife I killed weeks ago. I will transform their bodies and organs to show the world my hidden talents.

Animal couldn't take it no more, he'd come across a lot of crazy people. He even lived with the fact he wasn't wrapped too tight, but this was overboard.

Boom! Boom! Boom! Boom! Boom!

Animal killed Torres and got the fuck out of there so he could go meet Chloe for some morning sexy, but she hadn't been in the mood in the last two days since she found out about her mother's murder.

Chloe had cameras all over her mom's house so when she showed Animal the gruesome murder, he told her it was Jenny but the white woman he'd never seen before. He promised her he would take care of Jenny real soon.

Chapter 30

Little Haiti, Dade County

Hitler was parked next to a mailbox in his Chevy Impala he'd recently brought because the Hellcat was a dead giveaway and it was a Chi-Town thing everybody had a Camaro or Hellcat to outrun the police.

He watched Luc and Boss walk into a small house with a couple of goons, but Hitler knew there were goons throughout the house. Hitler knew he had to make a decision now, he saw Luc's driver sitting in his Bentley truck waiting on him to come out.

It was a bright, nice, warm day outside. *A perfect day for killing,* Hitler thought.

There was an empty SUV truck parked behind the Bentley which belonged to Luc's goons.

When Hitler saw Luc and Boss step out of the house, he made his way out of the car with his .50 Cal in his hand with 30 rounds. Luc and Boss climbed in the truck but when they heard shots being fired, they looked out the windows to see Hitler knocking down their guards one by one.

Boss pulled his gun out about to hop out until Luc stopped him. "It's good," said Luc.

The Bentley SUV rolled off slowly, leaving four dead Haitians on the pavement. Bullets started to hit the windows and doors, but nothing was happening.

"It's bulletproof," Luc said calmly lighting a Cuban cigar as Boss watched Hitler get in an Impala.

Hitler cursed at himself for not acting earlier when he saw Boss walk out, but he knew he'd have his time again because he knew where Boss rested his head.

He had to make a stop at in Overtown to cop some new guns from a nigga he'd met days ago in a strip club. When the crip nigga told him that he had guns for sale for the low Hitler was all ears.

Candice texted him asking him to meet her in South Beach in thirty minutes and he told her yes right after he made a stop.

Things with Candice had been amazing, he even moved in with her last month, but his time had been limited because he was busy trying to get Boss and Lil BD.

He pulled up to a small apartment complex and called his new gun plug.

***

South Beach, FL

Candice laid on the beach in her tanning chair, catching some sun in her bikini hugging her perfect body that most women would die for. She was waiting for her boo to arrive, she looked down the beach and saw him coming her way in shorts, a tank top, and flip flops.

"I see you're getting used to Miami heat?" she said staring at his dick print, smiling.

"I have no choice. Why you out here alone?" he asked sitting down in the chair next to her.

"I just wanted to get a quick tan and spend some time with you."

"Is that right?" he said, kissing her soft juicy lips.

He loved looking at her, there were very few women who could fuck with her, so he was glad to have her.

"You have fun today?" she asked.

"Huh?" he added caught off guard.

"In Little Haiti," she replied, putting on her shades blocking the sun from her eyes.

"How do you know I was in Little Haiti?"

"I know who you are and I'm okay with that. I just want to know why the Haitian Mafia? They're very dangerous and I don't want to see you get hurt, babe. You mean a lot to me already," she said seeing his face froze up.

"What else you know about them?"

"Nothing much, but I can help you," she said, making him laugh.

"You just focus on school, I'll handle the streets. How did you catch on?"

"While you were sneaking out of the house late at night thinking I was asleep, I was following you. I have a locator on your phone so when I saw who you were after I put two and two together," she said.

"You really thought I was fucking another bitch?"

"Of course, papi, you was doing too much. But my family are powerful people, so I can squeeze some info out of them. I hear there is a very big war going on, right now. I just want you to be ahead of your game," she said.

"I will. Now, let's go get some ice cream," he said, changing the subject, he was never the pillow talker type.

***

Downtown Miami

"Y'all can wait in the truck, I don't need a gang of dread heads coming in a supermarket with me," Jenny said placing her baby in a baby carriage handing him a baby bottle.

Everywhere Jenny went Lil BD sent three goons with her just in case especially when his seed was out with her. Jenny loved the feeling of being a mommy, she always wondered how it felt to be a mother. The only thing that was rough on her was breastfeeding because her son could suck on her nipples for days.

Her breasts were always swollen and sore, milk would soak her bra leaking all day, it was annoying. She entered the frozen store to pick up some diapers, baby food, and toys for him to chew on.

Jenny walked around the store while her son Brandon was sipping on his baby bottle full of milk. She pushed the carriage down aisle four which was the baby section full of baby food, toys, diapers, clothes, and wipes.

She placed the emergency brakes on the carriage and placed it on the side of the infant mildly while she let a Spanish man pass

Romell Tukes

her. Jenny was looking for the correct diaper size for Brandon because last time she got a size too small.

Once she found the 16-24 weeks size, she grabbed four big packs of Huggies and placed them under the baby carriage. Jenny grabbed a few more items before she made her way to the cash register. While her items were getting rung up she saw three of her guards rushed inside the shopping center on alert.

"You okay?" a Haitian man with dirty, thick dreads and gold teeth said, approaching her.

"Yes. I thought I asked y'all to stay in the truck?" Jenny said, paying for her items in cash.

"Mayo was just seen driving away from here, we have to go," he replied, grabbing her bags.

Jenny heard the man's name while Lil BD and Boss were talking but she didn't think she was in harm's way. Outside they escorted her back to the truck in a rush. Jenny saw Brandon choking on the milk, she stopped and pulled the bottle out of his mouth. He continued to choke even after she picked him up and patted lightly on his back. She saw how worse it was getting and got nervous. Brandon started throwing up blood and green shit.

"Call for help!" she yelled knowing something was wrong.

Jenny looked at his baby bottle to see it wasn't his, she'd never seen it before. Brandon's face turned red and his oxygen cut off while Jenny gave him CPR, but he was already dead.

By the time EMS came, he was gone. At the hospital, the doctors told Jenny he was poisoned somehow and he'd already contacted child services. She was crying non-stop over losing her baby and thinking only if she would've turned around faster in the baby aisle to see Mayo switch the baby bottles with one full of rat poison and five other poison liquid chemicals.

Chapter 31

North Miami, FL

Hector Santos's funeral came out to seven hundred guests in the biggest Roman Catholic Church in Miami. The church was filled with drug lords, businessmen, government officials, family, friends, and enemies.

Lexus and Boss sat in the front listening to the ceremony given in Spanish for over five hours.

Since the death of her father Lexus had been on an emotional rollercoaster, her father was her life, he was her heart. Now he was gone she felt half empty if it wasn't for Boss comforting her, she would be in a harder place.

The funeral was delayed twice because of the tropical storms. Lexus eventually told Boss who her father really was, she thought he would be mad at her for keeping his status a secret but to her surprise Boss wasn't at all.

When the funeral was over, Mark and his goons were outside waiting on Lexus because Mark was against any type of funerals, he thought it was bad luck.

"Nice of you to come inside to show respect to my father," Lexus told Mark who was leaning on a blue Bugatti with tints.

"Me and your father talked about this day many times, only if you knew the half," Mark said.

"What do you want?" she asked not in the mood to talk to nobody today.

"You're the boss now, Lexus, you run the show. I came to make sure you're ready for our family meeting in two days in Colombia at your father's old home which is now yours."

"I'll be there, bye," she said rudely not really liking Mark.

"Okay, sorry about your loss. Hector was a father to me and I'm looking for his killers, right now. Stay safe and make sure you have guards with you."

"I have my husband with me."

"Did you tell him what's up?" Mark asked looking at Boss who he thought was just using Lexus for her wealth.

"I did and he understands but we have to go, I'll see you in Colombia."

"Good, but don't bring him with you because the other families are not too heavy on blacks—no offense. I forgot your name," Mark stated.

"Look here, Mark. Ty is my fucking husband and whoever don't like it can suck my dick," Lexus said walking off holding Boss's hand.

***

Bogota, Columbia

Janella woke up out of her sleep at midnight, both of the guards asleep and snoring. She pulled out a chicken bone sharpening it on the cement wall back and forth. This was her 20th day straight working on turning the chicken bone into an ice pick and tonight was her deadline.

When Chloe told her that she'd killed her father, she'd been planning an escape and the only way was making a weapon. She needed to uncuff her wrists and ankles and get past the two guards sitting outside her room.

She finally placed the sharp ice pick into the cuff key area while peeking at the guards who were still sleep.

"Come on," she said to herself playing with the keyhole trying to open it but it looked as if nothing was happening.

After five minutes of playing with the keyhole and playing with the cuffs, she felt the click opening the cuffs.

Janella was so happy tears rolled down her eyes, she tried to undo her ankle cuff which took only seconds to unlock.

"Yesss," she said then slowly got up gripping the sharp chicken bone like a jail shank.

She slid past one of the guards, but the other guard was a light sleeper, so he opened his eyes when he heard her footsteps.

Janella saw this and stabbed the guard in his neck sixteen times while covering his mouth so he wouldn't be able to wake up the other guard.

Not one for waiting around she took off down the dark tunnel bar footed in her gown. Janella ran for dear life while looking back to make sure she was still in the clear.

She was getting winded halfway down the hall but she could feel freedom. Before she could make it to the end tunnel where a ladder was, a man stepped out from a blind spot and slammed the butt of his assault rifle in her head knocking her out.

The man dragged her body back to her room stripped her and this time he chained her to a pole in the corner of the room.

***

Downtown Miami

Julianne was in an expensive hotel suite drinking wine out of her glass, looking out of her hotel windows at the beautiful night skyline.   She wore a white dress with a slit down the middle of her back and chest showing a lot of skin.

She hated to dress up, but she just wanted to show her ex-boy-friend Louis what he was missing. Louis was the first man she'd ever loved but when he broke her heart, she became a true savage and grew a hate for him.

There was no denying the fact that she still cared for him, but she didn't trust him at all; he was the snake of all snakes.

The knock at the door took her out of her daze before making her way to open the hotel door. She knew she could never be seen with him or her father would be pissed.

Victor didn't even know about their past love relationship, if he did it would have been a big problem because not only was he against his daughter being with black men but he was a firm believer in never having any sexual dealing with anybody in an organized crime family.

"Hey," she said, opening the door to see him in a white Michael Kors suit with flowers in his hand looking handsome.

"You're wearing that dress," he said looking at her curves and breasts trying to control his manhood.

"These for me?" she said taking the roses and smelling them, then letting him inside.

"Yep," he said watching her toss them in the trash as he knew she would.

"The bar is over there. I know how much you like that white Henny stuff," she said pointing to the bar near the terrace.

"This is a nice place."

"Enough of the small talk, Louis. Did you get the shit I sent to your location?" she asked sitting down, crossing her legs and showing her meaty thighs.

"Yes, I did thank you so much. I promise I will pay you back," he said sitting across from her, sipping on his drink, admiring how thick she'd gotten.

"Keep your broken promises, papi. But there is one way you can repay me with the only thing you was ever good for," she said, cocking her legs open showing her phat pussy and loose pussy lips flop.

Louis already knew what she wanted, some head and dick, so it was a fair win. He gulped the drink and got between her legs and went to work. He sucked her stretchy pussy lips while fingering her making her moan crazy.

He put his tongue in and out of her pussy and sucked her clit until she climaxed four times shaking and quivering.

"Shittt!" she yelled, pushing him out of her pussy.

Louis started to strip down, ready to fuck, she had an ugly pussy, but it was tight and good.

"You can leave now, thank you we're even," she said fixing her dress and seeing how horny he was.

Louis was upset as he got dress, she led him out and slammed the door on him.

Chapter 32

South Beach, Miami

"This nigga tripping, bro. You see this shit?" Lil BD said to Malik as they watched Mayo look over his shoulders before entering a transgender club.

"Yeah, this shit wicked. We beefing with a killer homo gangsta," Milak replied, looking at the small club across the street on the South Beach strip full of clubs and bars.

"Won't be the first," Lil BD replied referring to years ago when they killed Fame.

"Hopefully it's the last," Malik replied watching Mayo's driver pull the Bentz truck to the side alley of the club.

"Facts."

"Aye man, I'm sorry about your seed," Malik said, seriously feeling the pain he was going through.

"Thanks, I knew I shoulda kept Jenny in Chicago. I be feeling as if it's all my fault. Burying your own child is a feeling I never thought I would have to experience," Lil BD said sadly.

"I like having you around. I wish you could have been down with me and your brother from day one. I had no clue you was a savage," Malik said.

"I wanted to pave my own way. I knew Boss was in the field checking a bag but I had no clue he was a Chi'Raq Gangsta. Y'all niggas names were ringing through the city," Lil BD said seriously watching drag queens come in and out the club Mayo walked into.

"Shit it was your brother's idea to start the crew, just so happens I lost my job. Animal's bitch ass come home and we just went in full blast," Malik said, reminiscing on days he was causing terror in Chi Raq.

"How long you think he's going to be in there?"

"I don't know." Malik watched the club side door in the alley.

***

Mayo exited the side door of the trans strip club with two Spanish Trannies who looked like female models but under their dresses were horse dicks. The last time he came to this club he had no clue it was a gay club until after he got some head and fucked a tranny he'd met in the club.

After he killed the tranny Mayo regretted it because the head and ass was on point, he never knew he was gay but now he was addicted.

Mayo climbed in the Benz truck with his guests ready for a long night at his condo. He saw two homeless men walk into the dark alley looking inside the dumpster, but he paid them no mind as one of his guests undid his pants, taking his dick down her throat.

Tat! Tat! Tat! Tat! Tat! Tat! Tat! Tat! Tat!

Bullets shattered the windows and door frames killing the driver and one of the trannies.

Mayo pushed the other tranny out of the Benz and started firing back but missing his shots. Lil BD shot him twice in his back making Mayo fall. Malik shot the other tranny eight times with his Draco.

"Ahhh!" Mayo yelled in pain reaching for his gun that was in front of him.

Lil BD fired fourteen rounds in the back of his skull. Lil BD and Malik raced back to their getaway car and pulled off before anyone saw them.

***

Havana, Cuba

Nandez took off his cowboy hat and looked around his beautiful horse ranch he'd built ten years ago on his 72 acres of land.

Three of his Arabian horses awaited him and his men so they could go on their daily horse ride through a deep trail in the woods on his land.

Growing up Nandez's dream was to be a horse jockey and train horses but life had a different approach.

Nandez saddled up on top of the horse and his two goons followed his lead on their horses. The trail was a long ride North so Nandez took his time enjoying the wildness this was his getaway.

Since the death of this brother Torres, he'd been staying in Cuba until he came up with a master plan to seek revenge for the murder of his brother. He knew Torres wasn't all the way wrapped too tight, but he was still his beloved brother.

The two guards behind him trailed close until one of them fell off making the guard stop in his tracks.

Psst! Psst! Psst!

The second guard was hit by a sniper also knocking him off the horse.

Nandez heard the horses behind him screaming which made him stop to look back. When he saw both of his men dead, he knew there was an active sniper somewhere. He kicked his horse and raced through the woods.

Psst! Psst! Psst! Psst! Psst! Psst!

The horse stopped and fell to the ground after being shot in the chest and thighs. Nandez went down with the horse. Three bullets entered his shoulder making him howl in pain. The sniper approached him dressed in a camouflage outfit that blended in with the trees and wildlife.

"Nandez, good to see you, pa," Chloe said walking up to him with her rifle pointed at him.

"Chloe, I knew this day would come," he said wiping the tears from his face because he wasn't ready to die.

"So long," she replied, shooting him five times in his face.

Chloe knew he went horseback riding twice a week at the same time on the same trail, so she decided to pay him a visit personally.

***

Miami, FL

Keith arrived in Miami at a Miami Port full of cargo and shipments coming in and going out. Keith was Trinidadian and part of the Trinidad Mafia ran by his sister Kamla and older brother Rawley.

Once a month Keith would bring a shipment of coke, heroin, and cannabis to Miami for their people to distribute drugs to other states and cities.

Seven dark-skinned men with pistols and shotguns patrolled the area making sure Keith was well protected. Keith saw a quick shadow race past his left making him pull out his gun. Shots started to ring out from all over the place from gunmen on top of cargo's and behind them.

"Fuck!" Keith yelled seeing four of his men bleeding to death on the ground.

Bloc! Bloc! Bloc! Bloc!

Keith shot two gunmen coming from his left taking them down. Keith didn't know where to go. He was unaware of the gunmen above him until the shooter took out the rest of his team.

Keith had to play for himself now, so he ran left only to run into Louis and nine goons with guns pointed at him.

"Nice shot, Keith, but not good enough. Why did your family rob me?"

"Fuck you."

"Okay, fair enough, we even anyway. I got your shipment, anyway, thank you" he said shooting Keith in the chest and stomach over twenty times starting a war.

Chapter 33

North Miami, FL

Jenny got up at four a.m. to start her day just as she's been doing since she was a teenager. Lil BD was knocked out sleeping, having consideration she slowly slid out of the bed to get dressed in her running gear. Once she was dressed, she made her way to the kitchen to get herself a cup of warm Colombian coffee. Since the loss of Brandon, she'd been very unstable, but she managed to stay strong and hold her head high.

After eating a protein bar and drinking her coffee, she was ready for her seven-mile run through a park around the corner from their condo. Once outside she stretched her limbs preparing for her run while looking at the dark morning skies.

Jenny placed her earbuds in her ear to listen to Nipsey Hussle's album on her pod and started running. Being tone and fit was a big part of Jenny's life. She was heavy on fitness and taking care of herself. She was trying to get Lil BD in shape because he was getting fat and letting himself go like most people did when they were overwhelmed with worldly events.

Jenny jogged through the park with her ponytail swinging from side to side. She was running on a cement path made for runners only. Her Nike running shoes came unloose almost making her trip over herself. She stopped to tie them but when she looked up a thick slab of pipe was coming down over her head.

Whack!

The sound of the pipe smashing her head sounded like metal cracking against a cement wall. Jenny had blood leaking from her face as she tried to get up.

"You shoulda never crossed me, Jenny!" Animal yelled before hitting her with the pipe again and again until she was unresponsive and dead.

Animal left her body between some trees and left a large blood trail so he knew it would only be a matter of time before her body was found. He knew she lived somewhere around the area from

Chloe's sources. He knew Jenny used to run a track every morning in the park up the block from where they both lived in Chi-Town. This was the first place he knew she would come if his source was correct.

Two days ago, he'd stalked the park to see her come every morning at the same time and today was no different. He knew today was the perfect time to make his move and when she stopped right in front of him it was a sign from up above for him.

***

Miami Beach, Fl

Weeks Later

Lexus was taking a swim in the backyard pool, enjoying some time alone while Boss was out looking for a mansion because for some reason he wasn't comfortable staying at her family mansion.

She climbed out of the pool in a bikini, soaking wet, and put her robe on thinking about what she was going to have the maids cook for dinner.

Mark walked out the back of the house with an upset facial expression and a folder in his hand.

"Lexus, we have a big issue," he said as she sat down crossing her legs.

"What is it?"

"Did you know your husband is a part of the Haitian Mafia?" he said.

"What? Are you sure you have the right person?"

"Take a look at it yourself," Mark said, handing her the folder with photos of Luc, Francisque, and Boss all together.

"We also found out who killed your father," he said, handing her a picture of two men entering the Mayor's party in a busboy uniform.

"I know him," she said pointing at Malik.

"The other man is, Luc. Years ago your father killed his mother when the Haitians and us were at war. Then Francisque who I believe is your husband's grandfather, somehow killed your mom, aunty, and brother," Mark said, seeing the fire and pain in her eyes.

Lexus looked through the pictures and it was clear as day that Boss had strong ties to the Haitians.

"What does my husband have to do with my father's death?" she asked.

"He could have been the one who sent the hit who knows, but he is in on the opposite team. He plays a big part in all this. I will do some more research, but I think you should stay away from him until we can figure this shit out. I don't want you to get hurt. I believe he is a very dangerous man. I believe all the wars going on around the city may link to him and his crew," Mark said.

"I'm grown and I can make my own choices. Last time I checked I ran this family. You're dismissed," she said rudely thinking about the news she'd just heard.

Not in a million years would she have figured out that Boss was part of the Haitian Mafia, but it all started to make sense because he never talked about his family and she'd never met them. Her mind was racing so fast she had to close her eyes tight and take three deep breaths. Lexus got up and rushed to the grass area near a garden and vomited all over the grass.

She had to come up with a plan quick because her life could be in danger and to make matters worse this morning she'd found out that she was pregnant.

***

Dolroy Beach, FL

Julianne sat on the barstool alone drinking a cocktail, she was on her sixth drink. She was in a white people's bar enjoying herself, unlike in Miami where places were always overcrowded with tourists and college students.

She had to fly out to Texas in a couple of hours for a business meeting with a Texas gang she'd supplied with coke.

"Excuse me, bartender, can I have a double shot of Patron? Better yet, I'll take the whole bottle," a handsome light-skinned man, dressed in a suit and tie said as he pulled up a chair next to her.

"Someone trying to get wasted?" she said with a chuckle.

"Yeah, long day," the man said.

"That makes us both. Hi, I'm Julianne," she said.

"Mikey! Why you by yourself beautiful?" he said, grabbing the Patron bottle.

"I'm not no more, handsome." she flirted.

"What do you do for a living?" Mike asked looking at her thighs in her jeans and camel toe.

"How about we just skip the small talk and go in the back to fuck?" Julianne said looking at his shocked facial expression.

"Okay, lead the way," he said, watching her get up and sashay her hips into the women's bathroom.

Mikey followed her into the bathroom and locked the door. She pulled her jeans and thongs down and bent over on the sink giving him a full view. Mikey pulled out a pistol with a silencer and shot her three times in her face. Mikey, whose real name was Malik, made his exit out of the bar full of white people.

Chapter 34

North Miami, FL

Chloe waited in the public park sitting on a bench, watching little kids playing, and having fun on the playground. She was a little tired today because she and Animal were fucking all night. The couple had been unable to spend time together because they had so much going on but she made time to please her man and every time she did she put on a show like a true porn star.

Her goons were behind her in the parking lot area in a GMC truck watching their boss's every move as she waited for her anonymous caller to arrive. Yesterday Chloe got a call from an anonymous man telling her he could get her Boss for a small fee.

She gave him a time and location for the next morning in a public park just in case it was a set-up, she would be well prepared. She heard a loud car pulling up and roaring it was a Ferrari 488 Spider. It parked beside her Pagani Huayoa BC yellow Roadster. When she saw the handsome man walking toward her in a suit, she had no clue who he was, she just stared at him.

"You look more beautiful in person," the man said.

"Cute and flirtatious too bad I don't know who the fuck you are?" she clapped back.

"Where are my manners? I'm Louis from the Haitian Mafia."

Chloe wanted to pull her gun out and shoot him in the head that second. "What do you think is stopping me from killing you?" she said knowing who he was but had never seen his face.

"You see that van parked two cars away from that GMC truck full of your men? Those men are ready for me to even look wrong, so they can fry your ass," Louis replied looking at the little kids running around the park.

"I don't have time for games, what do you want and why would you give up your nephew? This seems too fishy," she said clearly.

"I only owed my father loyalty and when you killed him that all went out the window."

"I don't know what you are speaking of," she replied with an innocent look.

"I know but you did me a favor and helped me expand. My father was blocking me out of a lot of business opportunities, so thank you."

"I thought I was cold-blooded," she said.

"I can lead you to Boss, Lil BD, and Luc for my small fee?"

"Which is?"

"Your family makes a lot of money in Chicago and the Midwest. I want in, let me supply your family."

"We have coke."

"I want to supply heroin," he said.

She was in deep thought because she could use another heroin plug beside Victor.

"Okay, I can agree to that but when will we be able to push this plan forward?" she asked.

"Just give me a little time, I got it," he added.

"Whenever you're ready I'll be waiting," she said getting up while Louis looked at her fat ass in her tight dress.

"Damn," Louis replied.

"Mmmm, maybe one day you can get a taste but this thing has been known to drive niggas crazy," she said.

"I'm pretty sure it does. One last thing, make sure you give Janella a slow death," he said.

"I plan to and you're a piece of shit brother."

"I know," he said watching her walk off.

Once Louis saw that she was gone he made his way to his car, before he was able to cross the street an older Range Rover pulled up in front of him, then the unthinkable happened. Three masked men jumped out with SK assault rifles. One shot Louis in his leg. They grabbed him and forced him into the Range as all hell broke loose.

Louis men saw what was going on and started shooting at the Range killing one of the men before the Range pulled off with Louis in the back.

Bullets shot out the Range's thick tires making the Range slam into a light pole. Louis crawled out of the truck with one of the gunmen inches behind him trying to recover from the crash that had him dizzy.

Louis's goons fired over thirty shots into the gunmen while the other gunmen died off the crash of impact. They got Louis off the ground unaware of the four little kids they'd just killed on the playground.

***

GMG Casino, Miami

The casino was packed this weekend and Victor was here for his daily getaway and to also support his bad gambling habit. He'd already lost 470,000 in five hours back and forth between the blackjack table and the poker table. There was so much going on right now Victor needed a weekend to himself while he let Julianne run the show because she was well prepared.

The news of Mayo's death hit him hard he didn't see that coming but what he didn't understand was Mayo dying in a car full of transgenders in the back of a Tranny club. Victor was far from dumb he just thought he'd raised Mayo better than that.

"Another hit, sir?" the blackjack dealer asked.

"No, I'ma fold." Victor laid his hand out to only lose again. "I'll be back," Victor said, getting up to leave with his two personal guards behind him.

Victor had to go get some more money from his room because he would only bring down 500,000 at a time. On the way to the elevator, they saw a sexy, young woman standing there in a pink satin gown dress with her long hair down to her butt.

Even the security guard couldn't help but stare at the beautiful, young, Spanish woman.

"You enjoying your evening?" Victor asked her as he waited on the elevator to come down from the sixth floor above.

"Yes, I am, thank you. How about yourself?" she asked in her sweet voice.

"It's just not my day today," he replied.

"Every dog has their day."

"True indeed, young lady," Victor said, letting six people get off the elevator and all of them were pissy drunk.

"Lady's first."

"Spoken like a true gentleman," she said making her way into the elevator full of mirrors from every angle.

"Where you from?" Victor asked, pressing the penthouse floor while she pushed the eighth.

"Miami."

"Of course, I mean what Island? I can tell by your accent you're either Colombian or Cuban."

"I'm mixed, papi," she replied sliding into her purse pulling out a .357 handgun.

Lexus shot both of his guards in the back of their head then aimed it at Victor who was scared for his life.

"Who sent you? If it's about money, I have 2 million upstairs. Please—" he begged

"Everybody must go," Lexus said, firing two shots into his heart.

The elevator doors opened, and a couple stood on the 8th floor waiting but when they saw the crime scene, they both turned around before catching a bullet to the doom a piece leaving a mess in the hallway.

Chapter 35

Months Later

Little Haiti, FL

Luc recently opened a Caribbean restaurant in the middle of the hood filled with Haitian killers, thugs, Zoe pounds, and robbers. The small restaurant had an outside area for its guest and an outside kitchen. Today the restaurant was closed because Luc had a very important meeting.

Over thirty of his soldiers were surrounding the restaurant and block ready to turn shit into little Iraq. Luc saw six pink SUVs with tints pulled up in a row back to back with Trinidad flags hanging out the windows. A bunch of big, armed Trinidadian niggas got out of the trucks and looked around before they opened the door for a woman to step out.

The woman was cocoa brown and thick with big breasts, long blond hair, and so much jewelry she was putting the sun out of business. She wore a tight, mini dress, heels, and sunglasses. She was a dime piece with a big, soft booty. Kamla walked through the restaurant after she told her men to wait outside.

Kamla was the boss of the Trinidad Mafia and her brother Rawley was her muscle. Her little brother Keith was in training before Louis killed him months ago.

She was a deadly, dangerous woman but she was about peace until she was crossed. She grew up in Port of Spain and San Fernando in the slums where she had to learn to fend for herself and her brothers.

Her mother and father split but they still did the best they could even with her father moving to the states. Kamla's dad was a big-time killer who started the Trinidad Mafia with his brother Lennox.

When her father moved to the states Lennox raised Kamla, Rowley, and Keith to be killers and gangstas but when Francisque murdered Lennox they were left by themselves.

Kamla restarted the family from the ground up. Now they were one of the most feared families in the Caribbeans.

Kamla walked to the outside area where Luc sat, drinking. "You still drinking, I see. I guess some shit don't change?" she said sitting down watching him ice grill her.

"You gonna grill me or kill me, nigga?" she said, taking off her sunglasses showing her chinky eyes.

"Kamla, good to see you," Luc said surly.

"Don't sound like. This is a nice little spot in the wrong area, but nice," she said.

"Let's just get down to business."

"Luc, is that any way to talk to your ex-wife?" she said looking at him with her evil eye.

Kamla and Luc were in a toxic marriage for close to six years until they had to break shit off.

"Kamla?"

"Okay, Luc, your brother Louis got a death wish. Months ago he disrespected my Island and people by having his drugs sent to my cargo deck. At first, I didn't know it was his, but I took it anyway. Come to find out it was for Maloney."

"Maloney? It can't be, Louis would never deal with that crazy nigga."

"Well, he does. So, anyway, we got the shit months later, he caught Keith out here, killed him, and took our shipment. I had my people try to kidnap him recently but he got away. We've been out of your family hair for a while, Luc, and another war is not needed but don't force my hand," Kamla stated strongly.

"Kamla, my brother is a grown man. You could have had this sit down with him, not me. Louis is my blood so if anything fatal happens to him, I will have my brother's blood on my hands. If that happens everyone will feel my wrath, including you," Luc replied looking at her alluring beauty.

"I knew you wouldn't be level-headed. You're still the same," she said getting up to leave. "Just to let you know you're putting your loyalty into the wrong people. When you pet a snake, you have to beware of the venom," she said walking off.

Luc watched her big, juicy ass jiggle and thought back to when he used to tear her ass up.

***

Southside, Chi-Town

Iman Sa'id was the last man in the mosque tonight. He'd just finished reading his Qu'ran and taking some notes for his Jummah service he planned to give on Friday. He was sitting in his office relaxing when he heard someone come in the front door of the mosque as always.

Muslims would come into the mosque to pray at all times of the day because it was open 24/7. Some brothers were so devoted to their religion they would sleep there just to make the compulsory congregational prayers.

Iman Sa'id looked up to see a young man dressed in a suit and tie standing at his doorway.

"Ass-Salaam-Alaikum, brother. How may I help you?" He'd never seen him a day in his life.

"Nice to finally meet you," Louis said walking into the office.

"Who are you?"

"I'm a friend of Kamla's," Louis said, now getting his full attention as anger spread across his face.

"So, why you come here? Shouldn't you be somewhere else looking for her?"

"Yes and no. You see, Sa'id—"

"Iman Sa'id."

"Okay, whatever. Your daughter owes me her life, so the best place I could think of to collect is here, starting with the Trinidad legend," Louis said looking into his beany eyes.

"Back in my day if we had an issue with a nigga, we would handle it with them, not the parents. Your generation is a mockery," Iman Sa'id stated showing no bite of fear in his heart.

"They say every generation is like a recycle."

"Yeah, I lived my life and killed a lot of people. Now I have to go and face my true fears with the man above."

"I will too one day."

"You know they say a coward has nine lives. How many do you have left?" Iman Sa'id asked him a serious question giving him a strange look.

"It looks like I have more than you, right now," Louis replied, pulling out his Colt .40 chrome, black with a red beam attached.

"Indeed, young brother. May Allah forgive us both," Iman Sa'id stated before Louis shot him nine times in the upper body killing him.

***

Port of Spain, Trinidad

Days Later

Kamla was in her bed soaking her pillows with her tears thinking about the news she'd received earlier about her father's death.

Her father had been out of the game for years and was focused on Islam. She felt like it was her fault he was dead. She knew there could only be one person capable of doing this and that was Louis or Luc, but she knew Luc better than herself. He would never cross that line, but she vowed to get Louis and give him a slow death.

Chapter 36

Santiago, DR

Danilo was in his courtyard behind his mansion looking into the dark, gray skies. He couldn't let go of his daughter's death, he wanted answers through blood. Lela was his baby girl. She was everything to him and his favorite child.

He saw Pablo walk out the back of the house with his usual fast walk.

"What you doing out here?"

"Just clearing my head. Did you do what I ask of you?" Danilo asked.

"Yes, that's taken care of. I had my men dismantle his body on the island of Hispaniola."

"Good," Danilo replied in deep thought.

"You okay?"

"You have a daughter and then raise her into a good woman, only to have her killed. Then I'll ask you are you okay?" Danilo looked at Pablo's young face.

Pablo didn't say a word he just stood there understanding his boss and mentor's pain.

"I need you to do me a big favor."

"Anything."

"Since I gave my daughter to Luc and he didn't fulfill his promise, I want you to kill him and everything he loves," Danilo said.

Pablo couldn't believe what he was hearing. "Are you sure about that?"

"I wouldn't tell you to do it if I wasn't," Danilo replied seriously.

"You know this will start a big war with us and them?"

"Do it look like I give a fuck about a war? Put all business ties on hold until we take care of this."

"Yes, sir, I'm on it." Pablo walked off with a grin because he loved the art of war.

Danilo had been thinking about this decision for a while now and he knew the outcome could lead to a big war but he was ready for that.

***

North Miami, FL

Hitler had been in the shower for over an hour fucking Candice. He'd just finished fucking her on the wall with her legs wrapped around his waist.

Candice got on her knees and took him into her mouth, sucking the tip of his dick slowly tasting her juices. She bobbed her head, going deeper down his shaft working her thick lips and long tongue.

"Uhmmmm, yeah gurl," Hitler moaned, closing his eyes, feeling her suck the shit out of his dick like she'd never done before. She was deep throating his dick, going faster and faster and slurping on his pre-cum at the same time. "Damn," he cried, grabbing onto the shower rail feeling himself about to explode until she stopped. "It's like that?" he said watching her get off her knees and turn off the showerhead.

"I need part two in the bed. Come on, daddy," she said in her heavy Spanish accent.

Hitler and Candice walked into the bedroom connected to the bathroom in towels and saw fifteen guns on them.

"Ummmm," Chloe said looking at Hitler's six-pack and chiseled frame.

"Who are y'all?" Hitler said angrily that he'd got caught slipping.

"I'm Chloe of the Colombia Cartel. I come to see you, Hitler. We have a lot in common," she said looking at Candice wondering where she'd seen her before.

"What may that be?" he said looking around at all her shooters ready to kill.

"You mean who may that be? Lil BD, Boss, the Haitian Mafia sound familiar?"

"Maybe."

"Well, I want you to come and work for me."

"Bitch you lost your mind, I ain't—"

Bloc! Bloc! Bloc! Bloc! Bloc! Bloc! Bloc! Bloc! Bloc!

Chloe fired bullets into Candice's petite frame and watched her take her last breath, while Hitler held her in his arms almost in tears. The bond he'd built with her was like no other female he'd ever met. Hitler stood up now pissed that Chloe had just violated him and his lover.

"Get out and give me a minute with him alone now," Chloe told her guards, and they did as she said.

Once they cleared the room, she approached Hitler face to face.

"Look, I'm sorry about her, but I can make you a rich man and we can kill all your ops together. I've been watching you since Chicago, I need you on my team pleaseeee," she begged.

"You just killed my bitch. Why couldn't you just set up a fucking meeting like anyone else?" he asked looking into her beautiful face. There was something about her in her dress that got his dick hard and it showed through his towel.

"I'm different and don't worry about her," she said looking down at his dick then back at him.

"Oh, yeah?"

"Yeah, I can finish off where she left," Chloe said getting on her knees and snatching his towel off his waist. She attacked his dick with her mouth and sucked his dick at a slow pace.

"Uhhhh—oohhh," he moaned as he began face fucking her, roughly grabbing the back of her head and pumping it into his dick. He nutted deep down her throat while looking into her eyes.

Chloe laid him on the bed, lifted her dress, and rode his dick like a cowgirl.

Hitler felt her tight pussy walls hug his dick while holding onto her phat ass, spreading her cheeks apart. Seconds later, they both came on each other out of breath, getting themselves together.

"You got some good dick."

"You got some good pussy," he replied.

"Get dressed," Chloe said.

"Where are we going?"

"Just come on."

"What about her?" Hitler said pointing at Candice's dead body.

"My men will clean it up to make it look like nothing happened," she said looking at Hitler stare at her thick curves. They left the crib together on a mission.

***

Dade County, Miami

Malik drove a black on black McLaren Senna through the dark streets on his way to meet Boss. The past couple of months things had been very weird for the crew, it felt like they were beefing with the whole city.

The news of Victor's death saved them a lot of trouble, so now all they had to worry about was Chloe.

Malik had to give it to Chloe. She was above smart, she did dirt and disappeared until it was time to show her face again.

Kylie wanted so bad to go on more and more missions. It was starting to scare him a lot, he was seeing a crazy side to her. He feared the same thing that happened to Jenny would happen to her if she didn't slow down.

Malik saw an undercover cop car pull up behind him and flash his lights.

"Shit," Malik said, pulling out his chrome and black Glock .45 placing it inside of his glove compartment. He pulled over by an elementary school parking lot. A uniform police officer climbed out with a bright flashlight pointing it at the driver's side window.

The officer tapped the flashlight on Malik's window. "How may I help you, officer?" Malik said, rolling down the window. "Is that you—"

Boc! Boc! Boc! Boc!

The officer shot Malik in the head four times, leaving him slumped in his driver's seat. The cop climbed back into the blue Crown Vic and raced off making a U-turn.

Once Lexus was blocks away, she slowed down thinking about what she'd just done. Lexus heard Boss tell Malik to meet him in Dade Canty at 11:30 p.m. So Lexus followed Malik from his condo. She planned to kill everybody involved in her father's death.

Lexus was pregnant but she wasn't showing yet nor had she told Boss yet. She'd been keeping a small distance from him because she still didn't fully know his part in her father's death but if he had anything to do with it, she had plans for him.

Chapter 37

Dade County, Miami

Boss was waiting for Malik to arrive at the junkyard so he could tell him about the lead he had on Chloe. Boss found out from a Haitian real estate agent that Chloe has a mansion in Miami Beach.

He checked his Richard Miller watch, seeing that Malik was twenty minutes late. Boss called him for the seventh time and it just kept ringing. Boss turned to leave but when he saw a truck coming at him full speed with the lights off, he panicked and dived on the ground.

Gunmen hopped out and shot him twice in his shoulder. "Ahhh!" Boss yelled while the men placed cuffs on him and took him away.

***

Bogota, Colombia

Boss was cuffed and tied to a chair inside a large room with haystacks that looked like a small barn. He was in extreme pain in both of his shoulders, as he tried to move around. The doors to the barn opened and he saw Animal and Chloe walk inside with big smiles on their faces.

"Boss, my nigga, you still look like money," Animal said standing in front of him with Chloe beside him in a turtle dress and heels.

"Fuck you, bitch," Boss said before Animal punched him in his face twice.

"Nice to finally meet you, Boss. This day has been due for some time now," Chloe said.

"Suck my dick," Boss spat.

"I would love to, but you have more problems to worry about," Chloe said

"What the fuck you mean you would love to?" Animal said, sounding as if he felt some type of way.

183

"Get a grip on yourself," she said.

"Let me hurry up and end you," Animal said, pulling out his gun and aiming at Boss. "Bye-bye," Animal said.

Boom! Boom! Boom!

Chloe watched Animal's body fall onto the ground with three big holes in his head. Boss looked at Chloe confused and bewildered.

"It's a long story, but I'm sure someone else can explain it better than I can," Chloe said, walking off to open the barn door to let someone in.

When Boss got a good view of the person's face, he thought he was seeing a ghost.

"Son, it's good to see that you've joined me," said Ty, Boss's father who he thought he killed years ago. "I know it's a surprise but close your mouth," Ty said approaching Chloe and kissing her on her lips. Ty kicked Animal's lifeless body twice.

"How?" Boss asked.

"How did I survive your headshot? Easy you missed the nerve when you tried to kill me. When the police arrived, I was still alive, kid. Number one rule of the game is to always kill your enemy. I know you're wondering how me and Chloe are connected?" Ty said looking at Chloe, blushing.

"No, I really don't care. Where is my mom?" Boss said.

"I'll get to that but me and Chloe have been a couple since high school. I was cheating on Janella with her. Can you blame me? Look at her. Anyway, she was my plug at one-point until our love life fucked up our business affairs. When I came home, she had a plan, and I was down with it, but our only issue was the Chi' Raq Gangstas. It was Chloe's idea to kidnap Janella. She's still alive for now, but we had no clue she was the daughter of Francisque, did we baby?" Ty asked Chloe who shook her head no.

"You're boring me," Boss said, yawning.

"Everything turned out just like we planned. This is where me and you part son, take care," Ty said pulling out a handgun pointing it to Boss's temple.

"You was always a piece of shit dad."

"Thank you," Ty said.

Tat! Tat! Tat! Tat! Tat! Tat!

Ty's body was riddled with bullets. Janella popped up from behind a haystack with a Mac 11. Chloe took off because Janella was rushing toward her shooting like a madwoman. Janella fired ten more rounds into Ty's body then rushed to Boss and untied him. She dug in Ty's pocket for the cuff keys and found them.

"Mom, oh my God! We gotta get out of here," he said once he was uncuffed.

He hugged her tightly, then they ran out of the barn and climbed into the jeep parked outside.

"There is a lot of shit I have to tell you. But we're about to be faced with a bigger problem," Janella said, driving off Chloe's estate as shots could be heard from Chloe's property towards the jeep.

To Be Continued...
Chi'Raq Gangstas 4
Coming Soon

Submission Guideline

Submit the first three chapters of your completed manuscript to ldpsubmissions@gmail.com, subject line: Your book's title. The manuscript must be in a .doc file and sent as an attachment. Document should be in Times New Roman, double spaced and in size 12 font. Also, provide your synopsis and full contact information. If sending multiple submissions, they must each be in a separate email.

Have a story but no way to send it electronically? You can still submit to LDP/Ca$h Presents. Send in the first three chapters, written or typed, of your completed manuscript to:

LDP: Submissions Dept
Po Box 944
Stockbridge, Ga 30281

DO NOT send original manuscript. Must be a duplicate.

Provide your synopsis and a cover letter containing your full contact information.

Thanks for considering LDP and Ca$h Presents.

BOW DOWN TO MY GANGSTA
By Ca$h
TORN BETWEEN TWO
By Coffee
THE STREETS STAINED MY SOUL II
By Marcellus Allen
BLOOD OF A BOSS VI
SHADOWS OF THE GAME II
TRAP BASTARD II
By Askari
LOYAL TO THE GAME IV
By T.J. & Jelissa
IF LOVING YOU IS WRONG... III
By Jelissa
TRUE SAVAGE VIII
MIDNIGHT CARTEL IV
DOPE BOY MAGIC IV
CITY OF KINGZ III
By Chris Green
BLAST FOR ME III
A SAVAGE DOPEBOY III
CUTTHROAT MAFIA III
DUFFLE BAG CARTEL VI
HEARTLESS GOON VI
By Ghost
A HUSTLER'S DECEIT III
KILL ZONE II
BAE BELONGS TO ME III

A DOPE BOY'S QUEEN III
By **Aryanna**
COKE KINGS V
KING OF THE TRAP II
By **T.J. Edwards**
GORILLAZ IN THE BAY V
3X KRAZY III
De'Kari
THE STREETS ARE CALLING II
Duquie Wilson
KINGPIN KILLAZ IV
STREET KINGS III
PAID IN BLOOD III
CARTEL KILLAZ IV
DOPE GODS III
Hood Rich
SINS OF A HUSTLA II
ASAD
KINGZ OF THE GAME VI
Playa Ray
SLAUGHTER GANG IV
RUTHLESS HEART IV
By Willie Slaughter
FUK SHYT II
By Blakk Diamond
TRAP QUEEN
By Troublesome
YAYO V
GHOST MOB II
Stilloan Robinson

KINGPIN DREAMS III

By Paper Boi Rari

CREAM II

By Yolanda Moore

SON OF A DOPE FIEND III

By Renta

FOREVER GANGSTA II

GLOCKS ON SATIN SHEETS III

By Adrian Dulan

LOYALTY AIN'T PROMISED III

By Keith Williams

THE PRICE YOU PAY FOR LOVE III

By Destiny Skai

I'M NOTHING WITHOUT HIS LOVE II

SINS OF A THUG II

By Monet Dragun

LIFE OF A SAVAGE IV

MURDA SEASON IV

GANGLAND CARTEL IV

CHI'RAQ GANGSTAS IV

By **Romell Tukes**

QUIET MONEY IV

EXTENDED CLIP III

By **Trai'Quan**

THE STREETS MADE ME III

By **Larry D. Wright**

IF YOU CROSS ME ONCE II

ANGEL III

By **Anthony Fields**

FRIEND OR FOE III

By **Mimi**

SAVAGE STORMS III

By **Meesha**

BLOOD ON THE MONEY III

By **J-Blunt**

THE STREETS WILL NEVER CLOSE II

By **K'ajji**

NIGHTMARES OF A HUSTLA III

By **King Dream**

THE WIFEY I USED TO BE II

By **Nicole Goosby**

IN THE ARM OF HIS BOSS

By **Jamila**

MONEY, MURDER & MEMORIES III

Malik D. Rice

CONCRETE KILLAZ II

By **Kingpen**

HARD AND RUTHLESS II

By **Von Wiley Hall**

LEVELS TO THIS SHYT II

By **Ah'Million**

MOB TIES II

By **SayNoMore**

BODYMORE MURDERLAND II

By **Delmont Player**

THE LAST OF THE OGS II

Tranay Adams

FOR THE LOVE OF A BOSS II

By **C. D. Blue**

Available Now

RESTRAINING ORDER **I & II**
By **CA$H & Coffee**
LOVE KNOWS NO BOUNDARIES **I II & III**
By **Coffee**
RAISED AS A GOON I, II, III & IV
BRED BY THE SLUMS I, II, III
BLAST FOR ME I & II
ROTTEN TO THE CORE I II III
A BRONX TALE I, II, III
DUFFLE BAG CARTEL I II III IV V
HEARTLESS GOON I II III IV V
A SAVAGE DOPEBOY I II
DRUG LORDS I II III
CUTTHROAT MAFIA I II
By **Ghost**
LAY IT DOWN **I & II**
LAST OF A DYING BREED I II
BLOOD STAINS OF A SHOTTA I & II III
By **Jamaica**
LOYAL TO THE GAME I II III
LIFE OF SIN I, II III
By **TJ & Jelissa**
BLOODY COMMAS I & II
SKI MASK CARTEL I II & III
KING OF NEW YORK I II,III IV V
RISE TO POWER I II III

COKE KINGS I II III IV
BORN HEARTLESS I II III IV
KING OF THE TRAP
By **T.J. Edwards**
IF LOVING HIM IS WRONG…I & II
LOVE ME EVEN WHEN IT HURTS I II III
By **Jelissa**
WHEN THE STREETS CLAP BACK I & II III
THE HEART OF A SAVAGE I II III
By **Jibril Williams**
A DISTINGUISHED THUG STOLE MY HEART I II & III
LOVE SHOULDN'T HURT I II III IV
RENEGADE BOYS I II III IV
PAID IN KARMA I II III
SAVAGE STORMS I II
By **Meesha**
A GANGSTER'S CODE I &, II III
A GANGSTER'S SYN I II III
THE SAVAGE LIFE I II III
CHAINED TO THE STREETS I II III
BLOOD ON THE MONEY I II
By J-Blunt
PUSH IT TO THE LIMIT
By **Bre' Hayes**
BLOOD OF A BOSS **I, II, III, IV, V**
SHADOWS OF THE GAME
TRAP BASTARD
By **Askari**
THE STREETS BLEED MURDER **I, II & III**
THE HEART OF A GANGSTA I II& III

By **Jerry Jackson**

CUM FOR ME I II III IV V VI

An **LDP Erotica Collaboration**

BRIDE OF A HUSTLA **I II & II**

THE FETTI GIRLS **I, II& III**

CORRUPTED BY A GANGSTA I, II III, IV

BLINDED BY HIS LOVE

THE PRICE YOU PAY FOR LOVE I II

DOPE GIRL MAGIC I II III

By **Destiny Skai**

WHEN A GOOD GIRL GOES BAD

By **Adrienne**

THE COST OF LOYALTY I II III

By Kweli

A GANGSTER'S REVENGE **I II III & IV**

THE BOSS MAN'S DAUGHTERS I II III IV V

A SAVAGE LOVE **I & II**

BAE BELONGS TO ME I II

A HUSTLER'S DECEIT I, II, III

WHAT BAD BITCHES DO I, II, III

SOUL OF A MONSTER I II III

KILL ZONE

A DOPE BOY'S QUEEN I II

By **Aryanna**

A KINGPIN'S AMBITON

A KINGPIN'S AMBITION **II**

I MURDER FOR THE DOUGH

By **Ambitious**

TRUE SAVAGE I II III IV V VI VII

DOPE BOY MAGIC I, II, III

MIDNIGHT CARTEL I II III

CITY OF KINGZ I II

By **Chris Green**

A DOPEBOY'S PRAYER

By **Eddie "Wolf" Lee**

THE KING CARTEL **I, II & III**

By **Frank Gresham**

THESE NIGGAS AIN'T LOYAL **I, II & III**

By **Nikki Tee**

GANGSTA SHYT **I II &III**

By **CATO**

THE ULTIMATE BETRAYAL

By **Phoenix**

BOSS'N UP **I , II & III**

By **Royal Nicole**

I LOVE YOU TO DEATH

By Destiny J

I RIDE FOR MY HITTA

I STILL RIDE FOR MY HITTA

By **Misty Holt**

LOVE & CHASIN' PAPER

By **Qay Crockett**

TO DIE IN VAIN

SINS OF A HUSTLA

By **ASAD**

BROOKLYN HUSTLAZ

By **Boogsy Morina**

BROOKLYN ON LOCK I & II

By **Sonovia**

GANGSTA CITY

By **Teddy Duke**
A DRUG KING AND HIS DIAMOND I & II III
A DOPEMAN'S RICHES
HER MAN, MINE'S TOO I, II
CASH MONEY HO'S
THE WIFEY I USED TO BE
By Nicole Goosby
TRAPHOUSE KING **I II & III**
KINGPIN KILLAZ I II III
STREET KINGS I II
PAID IN BLOOD **I II**
CARTEL KILLAZ I II III
DOPE GODS I II
By **Hood Rich**
LIPSTICK KILLAH **I, II, III**
CRIME OF PASSION I II & III
FRIEND OR FOE I II
By **Mimi**
STEADY MOBBN' **I, II, III**
THE STREETS STAINED MY SOUL
By **Marcellus Allen**
WHO SHOT YA **I, II, III**
SON OF A DOPE FIEND I II
Renta
GORILLAZ IN THE BAY **I II III IV**
TEARS OF A GANGSTA I II
3X KRAZY I II
DE'KARI
TRIGGADALE I II III
Elijah R. Freeman

GOD BLESS THE TRAPPERS I, II, III

THESE SCANDALOUS STREETS I, II, III

FEAR MY GANGSTA I, II, III IV, V

THESE STREETS DON'T LOVE NOBODY I, II

BURY ME A G I, II, III, IV, V

A GANGSTA'S EMPIRE I, II, III, IV

THE DOPEMAN'S BODYGAURD I II

THE REALEST KILLAZ I II III

THE LAST OF THE OGS

Tranay Adams

THE STREETS ARE CALLING

Duquie Wilson

MARRIED TO A BOSS... I II III

By Destiny Skai & Chris Green

KINGZ OF THE GAME I II III IV V

Playa Ray

SLAUGHTER GANG I II III

RUTHLESS HEART I II III

By Willie Slaughter

FUK SHYT

By Blakk Diamond

DON'T F#CK WITH MY HEART I II

By Linnea

ADDICTED TO THE DRAMA I II III

IN THE ARM OF HIS BOSS II

By Jamila

YAYO I II III IV

A SHOOTER'S AMBITION I II

By S. Allen

TRAP GOD I II III

By Troublesome
FOREVER GANGSTA
GLOCKS ON SATIN SHEETS I II
By Adrian Dulan
TOE TAGZ I II III
LEVELS TO THIS SHYT
By Ah'Million
KINGPIN DREAMS I II
By Paper Boi Rari
CONFESSIONS OF A GANGSTA I II III
By Nicholas Lock
I'M NOTHING WITHOUT HIS LOVE
SINS OF A THUG
By Monet Dragun
CAUGHT UP IN THE LIFE I II III
By Robert Baptiste
NEW TO THE GAME I II III
MONEY, MURDER & MEMORIES I II
By Malik D. Rice
LIFE OF A SAVAGE I II III
A GANGSTA'S QUR'AN I II III
MURDA SEASON I II III
GANGLAND CARTEL I II III
CHI'RAQ GANGSTAS I II III
By Romell Tukes
LOYALTY AIN'T PROMISED I II
By Keith Williams
QUIET MONEY I II III
THUG LIFE I II
EXTENDED CLIP I II

By **Trai'Quan**
THE STREETS MADE ME I II
By **Larry D. Wright**
THE ULTIMATE SACRIFICE I, II, III, IV, V, VI
KHADIFI
IF YOU CROSS ME ONCE
ANGEL I II
By **Anthony Fields**
THE LIFE OF A HOOD STAR
By **Ca$h & Rashia Wilson**
THE STREETS WILL NEVER CLOSE
By **K'ajji**
CREAM
By **Yolanda Moore**
NIGHTMARES OF A HUSTLA I II
By **King Dream**
CONCRETE KILLAZ
By **Kingpen**
HARD AND RUTHLESS
By **Von Wiley Hall**
GHOST MOB II
Stilloan Robinson
MOB TIES
By **SayNoMore**
BODYMORE MURDERLAND
By **Delmont Player**
FOR THE LOVE OF A BOSS
By **C. D. Blue**

BOOKS BY LDP'S CEO, CA$H

TRUST IN NO MAN

TRUST IN NO MAN 2

TRUST IN NO MAN 3

BONDED BY BLOOD

SHORTY GOT A THUG

THUGS CRY

THUGS CRY 2

THUGS CRY 3

TRUST NO BITCH

TRUST NO BITCH 2

TRUST NO BITCH 3

TIL MY CASKET DROPS

RESTRAINING ORDER

RESTRAINING ORDER 2

IN LOVE WITH A CONVICT

LIFE OF A HOOD STAR

www.ingramcontent.com/pod-product-compliance
Lightning Source LLC
Chambersburg PA
CBHW070506260626
47161CB00004B/1478